Single
GIRL RULES
#AUCTIONED

USA TODAY BESTSELLING AUTHOR

IVY SMOAK

Single Girl Rule #5
Have wine in your purse at all times.

Chapter 1

BETTER THAN ODEGAARD
Sunday, Sept 22, 2013

I loved helping a fellow single girl out. *I'm a very selfless person.* But girl, it's honestly really hard for me to sit back and let another girl get all the dick.

Especially because beautiful cocks are one of my all-time favorite things.

That and shoes.

And of course my bestie Ash. Which is why I was currently high-tailing it away from all the 8-inch erections on Roma Island and back toward the yacht. I was on a mission. Save Ash from her dirty, hot kidnapper. And then get fucking railed. *Honestly…maybe by her kidnapper…*

I would love that for me. I bit my lip as I hit the gas harder on my jet ski. The combination of the vibrating jet ski seat and the idea of being taken by the kidnapper made me moan. Especially since I knew the kidnapper was the banana king. And boy was *packing.*

There was just something about a good kidnapping that really did something to me. Probably because I really loved being tied up and blindfolded. It heightened everything. Especially if it was legit a life-or-death scenario. Although, no one would kill me after they saw my perfect tits. So it wasn't that scary. #PerfectTitsFacts.

I was almost back to the yacht where my extraction team was. I was fashionably late as always, and I could see Ghostie staring at me. His strong arms were folded across his chest, a cute little scowl plastered to his face. Teddybear walked up next to him and looked equally strong and annoyed.

Hmm. I wondered if maybe I liked the idea of being kidnapped so much because of that little lesson that Ghostie and Teddybear had given me in the art of kidnapping. It wasn't really a lesson from them, so much as I coerced them into it and then blackmailed them into being at my beck and call for all my needs ever since. But the details weren't important. What was important was that Ghostie and Teddybear had really enjoyed showing me all the sexy things a kidnapper would do to my body.

That was the first time I'd had sex with my bodyguards. And I hadn't stopped since. They were like…obsessed with me. But as I stared at Ghostie's stern frown and Teddybear's piercing gaze, I felt myself smiling. Honestly, with the two of them around and my superior intellect and problem solving skills, I'd never truly be kidnapped. But I could sure act it out again…

Gah, there was no time. I had to save Ash. Apparently the banana king had moved up the sex auction. I was up against the clock instead of up against a cock. I needed to save Ash's virginity before it was too late.

I pulled my jet ski up to the yacht and Ghostie helped me on deck. I expected him to immediately get back to work, but instead he pulled me down a flight of stairs.

"Ghostie, what are you doing? We need to hurry and save Ash!"

He grunted a response, pulling me past one of the cabins and into a small hall bathroom. He locked the door behind us. The space was tight, almost as small as the restroom on Daddy's fun jet. But it seemed smaller since Ghostie was so muscular and domineering and currently caging me in against the vanity.

I put my hand on his chest. "Ghostie, we need to get to Ash before it's too late..."

"I lied. The sex auction wasn't moved up. I just needed you back here."

"Why?"

"Because I meant what I said on the comms. This..." He traced his thumb along my lower lip. "...Is *mine.*"

Before I could respond, he kissed me, slamming my butt against the edge of the vanity.

Fuck. It was like he'd just been on the vibrating jet ski instead of me. I was really loving how possessive Ghostie was getting. But he thought my mouth was his? *Silly Ghostie.* No man was ever going to own me. Honestly, it was much more likely that I'd one day own a man.

I remembered the sinful things Ghostie had whispered through the comms while I was back on the island. *If I was there, I'd tie your hands to the posts and bend you over.*

It was like he knew I wanted him to play kidnapper. I'd stared into the cameras the whole time I deepthroated another man. Ghostie had been watching. And I'd put on a good show for him. His ragged breath through my earpiece would have been enough for me to know he liked it. But he'd also said a few more things that had tipped me off.

Your mouth is mine.

I'll rail you until your legs go numb.

Oh, and then there was the obvious - *You better be ready for another cumshot when you get back to this boat.*

Ghostie's hands pulled at the fabric of my referee costume like he was a wild animal.

I thought maybe he'd cum watching me through the cameras. But apparently he'd been waiting for me.

One of his hands skated down to my exposed breast, while his other fell to my throat. His fingers tightened ever so slightly.

God yes.

He bit my lower lip before pulling back.

I tried to stand up on my tiptoes to further the kiss, but his hand around my neck kept me in place. *Just like a kidnapper would do…*

"On your knees, you little slut."

I smiled up at him. I loved when he spoke dirty to me. "I knew you liked what you saw me do back on the island." I reached out and unzipped his pants, palming his erection through his boxers.

He groaned.

"In fact, I think you loved every second of it."

His thumb pressed on the center of my throat. "On. Your. Knees."

Well, I did promise him I would. I'd been a little bit of a tease. And I couldn't violate Single Girl Rule #24: No blue balls allowed. Finish what you start.

But I also didn't want to ruin this kidnapper roleplay by acting too eager.

"Make me," I said.

He stepped forward, caging me in even more. His erection pressed against my stomach. "You have five seconds to get on your knees. Or I'll spank you so hard that you won't be able to sit down for days."

Was that a threat? Because that just sounded amazing to me. I never sat down for long periods of time any-way…unless I was sitting on a big cock.

"You wouldn't dare," I said.

He grabbed the thin straps that were the only thing holding my dress together. And then he pulled. The tug spun me around so hard that the front of my hips slammed into the vanity. My dress fell to a puddle on the floor around my high heels.

The palm of his hand landed hard on my right ass cheek. This was why thong bikini bottoms were so good. Because you didn't even have to get fully undressed to get a proper spanking. Justin must have known that when he designed my referee outfit. I couldn't wait to see the other outfits he'd put together for me.

But right now I was much more focused on Ghostie spanking me.

Yes, I loved Justin and my Odegaard outfits. But I think maybe I loved Ghostie's hands even more. Which was really saying something.

He spanked me again.

I'd already been wet. But the sting of his palm on my ass had me drenched. Each time my hips dug into the vanity I felt my pussy clench. Maybe I should have gotten on my knees. Because at least that way I could touch myself...

"On your knees," Ghostie said from behind me. "Now."

I turned around. But he was so close to me that there was really no room for me to follow his orders. So instead I grabbed his hand and lightly ran my tongue along his index finger before sinking the whole thing into my mouth.

"Fucking hell." He grabbed me around the waist and hoisted me up on top of the vanity. Then with one strong tug, he ripped my bikini bottom in half and sunk all eight inches of his cock deep inside of me.

Oh God. I loved getting what I wanted.

His pace was relentless. Punishing. Exactly how I liked it.

I pushed the back of his shirt up so I could dig my fingernails into the muscles of his back.

He grunted as I scratched his skin.

I was pretty sure he loved when I marked him just as much as I loved him marking me. His fingers were digging into my hips so hard I was sure I'd have bruises. Perfect little Ghostie thumbprint bruises. They'd look so hot lining the edge of a colorful thong.

"Harder," I moaned.

But I didn't need to ask. Ghostie was already thrusting harder. He knew how greedy I got when he was deep inside of me.

It was like my body was starved for sex. Which made sense, because I'd been handing out blowjobs all morning instead of getting properly satisfied. And Ghostie definitely knew how to satisfy me.

His fingers dug harder into my hips, pulling me in to match his powerful thrusts. I came so fast, pulsing around his thick cock. "Ghostie."

He groaned in response, slamming into me harder.

I tilted my head back and it hit the mirror. *Ow.* I smiled. This was the best sex I'd had in a small, confined space. So much better than having sex with Chad in Daddy's fun jet. If you could even call it that. #HisDickIsMinscule.

Fuck. I was going to come again. And I wanted Ghostie to cum too. "Use me," I panted, pretending he was my naughty kidnapper. "However you need me." I spread my thighs farther apart. The angle had me moaning again.

I expected him to pull out and explode all over me.

Instead he groaned and thrust even deeper. "Fuck," he said as he tensed and pulsed inside of me.

There was something seriously hot about a man losing control and pumping you full.

He slowly pulled out, some of his cum sliding down my thigh.

"I better clean up," I said. "I'm not sure how fuckable I'll look during phase 2 of the rescue mission if I already have cum dripping down my thigh." I ran my index finger through his cum and then licked it clean.

"Jesus," he said.

I smiled around my finger. He wanted me again. I could tell. "You know…I'm surprised you didn't wait until I changed into my maid uniform. It's so very short. And it really hugs my girls." I ran my wet finger between my naked breasts.

He lowered his eyebrows as he stared at me.

"Maybe you can whisper sinful things in my ear while you watch me again. Would you like that, you bad boy?"

He grunted a response.

I was pretty sure that meant, "Yes. And it's time for phase 2," in Ghostie speak.

Chapter 2

I MAKE MESS
Sunday, Sept 22, 2013

"Ready, girls?" I asked as our van pulled up to the service entrance of the Locatelli Resort and Spa.

"Yes, yes," said Slavanka.

"Sí," agreed Esme.

"Yeah you are. Those accents are on point. But more importantly, your tits look amazing in these maid uniforms." I honked each of their boobs twice and they honked mine back.

We'd gotten lucky that the banana king dressed his maids in super sexy uniforms. They had all the elements of a traditional French maid uniform – black skirt, frilly white bib, white collar, garters, stockings… You know, the usual stuff. But they also had puffy black sleeves slashed with white and a plunging V neckline. They were basically the world's sexiest mashup of a French maid and a Swiss Guard uniform.

Oh, and when Justin made his replicas, he'd added some underwire to *really* make our tits look outstanding. There was no freaking way any guards would be looking at our faces.

"What accent you do?" asked Slavanka.

"You know what…I think I'll do Russian."

"Really?" She looked so excited.

"Yes, yes," I said, perfectly copying her usual response.

Slavanka nodded in approval. "We save Ash now." She slid the van door open and got out.

Just as I'd hoped, the guard's eyes went straight to her long legs. And then to her tits. But never to her face.

Esme and I followed her out and started unloading half-a-dozen duffel bags from the back.

I was all ready to explain to the guard that something heinous had happened and a room on the 20th floor needed a *deep* cleaning, but he didn't bother to ask about all our bags. Probably because the bottom of my ass had been peeking out from under my skirt as I bent over to grab them.

"IDs please," he said as we approached the entrance.

I shifted one of the bags over my shoulder and pulled on my ID card to bring it up right in front of my cleavage.

He scanned it and waved me through.

God, I love my tits. They made everything in life so much easier. Especially getting past dumb guards who definitely should have realized that I was using a stolen ID card. I mean, yes, we'd done some quick work to change the name written on the card. But if he had gone back to his computer and checked, he would have seen that my ID was linked to a guard named Giuseppe Esposito.

Slavanka and Esme got past him just as easily.

We loaded our duffel bags onto maid carts, and then we split up.

Esme went to hide some supplies for us to use later, Slavanka went to infiltrate the command center, and I went to the bachelorette suite.

I knocked on the door.

There were excited giggles inside and I definitely heard the word *stripper* being thrown around. And then a very flustered redhead cracked the door open and peered out. Her pink sash identified her as the matron of honor.

She gasped and slammed the door in my face.

What the hell?

I knocked again. "Housekeeping!"

This time the bride answered the door.

"Sorry about that," she said. "My friend thought you were a stripper."

"No, no," I said in my Russian accent. "I maid."

"See?" called the bride back to her friends. "She's not a stripper. She's just the maid."

The redhead peeked around the corner. "Are you sure?" she whispered. "Her boobs are everywhere."

"Relax, Autumn," said a third girl in a maid of honor sash. She had a slight accent that made her sound hella fancy. "If I'd hired a stripper, it would have been a guy."

"But you didn't, right?" asked the redhead.

The maid of honor shrugged.

The redhead's eyes got even bigger.

"She's just messing with you," said the bride. "I think."

"Come on," said the maid of honor. "Quit talking to the help and let's open some presents."

The bride turned back to me. "Can you come back later?"

"Yes, yes," I said. "I clean bathroom." I disengaged the brake on my cart and pushed it into the suite.

"Ah!" yelled the redhead. "She's about to strip!" She covered her eyes and ran directly into a lamp.

I tried not to laugh. She reminded me so much of Ash. I know it had only been a little over a day since she'd been kidnapped, but I couldn't wait to have her back to safety. And then find someone to take her V-card.

"She's not gonna strip," said the maid of honor. "She just doesn't understand English."

I turned into the bathroom and shut the door behind me.

"I'm in the bathroom," I whispered into the comms.

"Copy that," said Ghostie. "Slavanka needs your help at the command center, so hurry it up."

"Got it. I'll be there in five."

I pulled both duffel bags off the cart. I hid the first one under the vanity, and then I unpacked the other. Just as I'd requested, it was filled with the ultimate collection of bride squad gear.

I carefully refolded each black monokini and put a matching pair of black Odegaard heels behind them on the vanity. Then I got to the bride's outfit.

Hot damn, Justin!

That boy sure knew what he was doing.

If he had been a basic ass bitch, he would have given her a white monokini in the same style as all the others.

But he was Justin, and he worked for Odegaard. So of course he'd freaking nailed it.

The neckline on the bride's monokini dipped way lower than the others. And to really make her stand out, he'd included white gloves, a garter, and a crown that spelled out BRIDE in diamond-studded letters.

I adjusted the crown a little bit to get the presentation perfect and then grabbed the final thing out of the duffel bag – a fancy piece of parchment with a printed note:

Here's a little something to help you celebrate your final weekend as a single girl.
XOXO
Your Future Husband

Perfect. I propped it up against the crown and stood back to admire my handiwork. The bride was gonna be SO excited when she found this.

I kind of wanted to stick around to see their reactions, but Slavanka needed my help. And anyway…this wouldn't be the last of my time with these girls. They were a crucial part of phase 4.

I jumped up onto the counter and loosened all the screws on the air vent. It still stayed in place, but if someone say…kicked it from inside the air duct later on in the rescue mission, it would pop right out. Once I was sure it was perfect, I ducked out of the bathroom and made my way up over to the command center.

Slavanka was waiting me for when I got off the elevator.

"What's the problem?" I asked.

"No computer in command room," said Slavanka. "Only screens."

"Well they must be somewhere."

"Yes, yes."

"They're in an adjacent room," said Ghostie into my earpiece. "And there are currently three guards in there."

"So what's the problem?" I asked. "It's easy to distract three men. And also quite fun."

Ghostie growled.

"Oh, I get it. You don't want me to get triple teamed until you have access to the cameras so you can watch, you naughty little boy."

"No," said Ghostie. "The command center has a camera watching all the servers. So one of you needs to distract the guard watching the monitors while the other one sneaks past the guards and uploads the virus."

Slavanka held up a thumb drive. "I upload virus."

"Alright then. I'll make sure no one in the command center sees you."

"Should you have a codeword for when the coast is clear?" asked Ghostie.

"No need. I'll watch the monitors and distract the guard at just the right time." I wheeled my cart over to the command center door and scanned my badge. The lock clicked open.

"Housekeeping!" I announced as I walked in. The guard didn't even look over at me.

But I definitely looked at him.

Just like all the other guards in this place, he gave off some serious big dick energy. And the way the sleeves of his tight black V-neck hugged his bulging biceps… *Yummy.*

I walked over and started dusting the counter next to his keyboard.

There were about thirty monitors spread out all over the wall, so it took me a little while to locate the one showing footage of Slavanka walking down a row of floor-to-ceiling metal cages housing the servers and wires. So. Many. Wires.

She looked around to make sure no guards could see her, and then she started to open one of the cages.

I reached up and dusted that screen so that the guard next to me couldn't see what she was up to.

"Hey," he said. "Don't block my view like that."

"Dust block your view?" I asked in my Russian accent. And then I started dusting the screen more vigorously.

"No. *You're* blocking my view."

I moved my feather duster just enough so that only I could see the screen. Slavanka was walking back down the row of servers, so I assumed she'd accomplished her mission.

"Oh. So sorry." I moved the duster. "We good now?"

"Yeah," said the guard.

But my question hadn't been for him. It had really been my sneaky way of asking Ghostie for confirmation that he'd gotten access to their system.

"Nothing yet," said Ghostie.

Hmm…

I looked back at the feed of Slavanka. She wasn't leaving the server room. In fact, it seemed like she was walking *towards* the guards.

I didn't know what she was up to. But I had a feeling it was time to escalate my distractions.

"Oh no," I said. "Screen so dusty. I clean." I leaned over the guard and started dusting one of the screens that was almost out of my reach. My tits were right in his face. And when I twisted just so, one of them popped out.

I actually heard him swallow.

Which was good. Because that meant he was staring at my tits instead of watching Slavanka pickpocketing one of the guards' keyrings.

I kept dusting the other screen as I watched her walk back to the server cages. But then the camera started to zoom up on her. And I was pretty sure it wasn't happening automatically.

"What is she up to?" the guard muttered as he fiddled with a joystick to zoom in more.

What the hell? Was this guard seriously more focused on his job than my naked boob in his face? My first thought was that he was gay, but even gay men liked my amazing breasts. So he must have just been such a stud that boobs didn't phase him anymore. And if he was getting tons of boobs even half as good as mine, then he must have been absolutely *packing.*

I quit dusting the screen and started to stand back up, but in the process I made sure to knock over his mug of coffee.

"Ah!" he screamed as the hot liquid splashed onto his lap.

I jumped back and pretended to be shocked by what I had done.

"Oh no," I said. "I make mess." I grabbed a roll of paper towels off my cart and started blotting his pants, paying extra attention to his increasingly hard cock.

He groaned a little as I rubbed the paper towels over his length.

Not bad at all.

I didn't know how big he'd be at full mast, but I could feel that he was already over eight inches.

"Pants too wet," I said. "Must remove." I unzipped them and yanked them down, being sure to take his boxers with them.

His huge cock sprung up and nearly hit me in the face.

I wasn't sure what Slavanka was up to, but Ghostie hadn't said anything to confirm that she'd accomplished her mission. So I had to assume that my distraction needed to continue.

I dabbed a paper towel against his erection.

"Oh no," I said. "Coffee get on your cock. I clean." I licked him from his base all the way to the tip. The richness of the coffee mixed with the saltiness of his precum was fucking delicious.

"Holy shit," he muttered as I wrapped my lips around his cock and slid all the way down, licking up every drop of coffee along the way.

I locked eyes with him as his cock entered my throat. And then I went even farther.

There was nothing better than looking into a man's eyes when his cock was buried in your throat. In that moment, I was his entire world. And he would never forget me. Sure, he'd be with a lot of other girls. But none of them would ever compare to the hot Russian maid who spilled coffee and gave him the best blowjob of his life.

I pushed his chair backwards so I could get an even better angle. Each flick of my tongue got him closer to the edge. Any second now, I was going to get my reward.

But then someone interrupted.

Chapter 3

MEANY MAN CRY LIKE BABY
Sunday, Sept 22, 2013

"What the hell?" said a deep voice from across the room.

"Oh shit," said the guard I was blowing. He pushed my head away from his cock and then covered himself.

I stood up and adjusted my bodice to put my tits away.

"Dude," said the new guy. "You know we aren't allowed to touch the maids. And speaking of maids...what's going on there?" He pointed to the screen where Slavanka was chasing a guard.

No! Don't look at that! "I spill coffee on lap," I said. "So I clean." I bit my lower lip and batted my eyelashes at him.

"Really?" asked the new guard. Now that he was staring at me, he seemed to forget about the screens behind me. "Because it sure looked like you were giving him a blowjob."

"Yes, yes. Chemicals too harsh for penis. I clean with mouth."

"Oh really? In that case..." He grabbed the flask off my maid cart and poured it all down the front of him.

Ah! I'd kept that flask near me ever since I'd read Single Girl Rule #5: Have wine in your purse at all times. I always knew it would come in handy, but I never expected it to happen quite like this.

"Oh no," I said. "You make mess. I clean?"

"You wouldn't mind?"

"No, no. It my job." I walked over and dropped to my knees as he unbuckled his pants. I got nice and close to make sure his cock hit me in the face when it popped free from his boxers.

I let out an excited little squeal.

And then I shoved him into my mouth. Wine paired with cock was even better than coffee and dick.

I swirled my tongue around his thick shaft as I locked eyes with the first guard.

One raise of my eyebrow was all he needed to get out of his chair and walk over to us.

"What are you doing?" asked the second guard.

"She wasn't done cleaning me."

"Oh well. It's my turn now."

I pulled the new guy out of my mouth and pushed his cock between my breasts. "I clean both?" I asked.

"How you gonna do that?"

I stood up and unzipped my dress. The black and white material fell to the floor, leaving me in nothing but gloves, stockings, and heels.

Both guys looked so excited.

"Who fuck me first?" I asked.

"Me," they both said. But the original guard made the first move, so my pussy was his. One of his hands went to my hips as the other bent me over. His stiff cock bounced against my ass and then he guided it into me.

Inch by inch.

Deeper and deeper.

Yes, I'd just been fucked by Ghostie a few hours ago. But each cock was so different. Ghostie was thick and veiny. But this guy was smooth and a little curved. And much gentler. It was almost like a massage for my insides. And like any proper massage, it came with a side of cock in my mouth.

It didn't take long for the men to get into a rhythm where one pulled me one direction, and then the other pulled me the opposite way.

There was nothing better than sliding back and forth on two thick cocks. Actually, that wasn't true. I could have had one in each hand. And maybe one in my ass like Karma had done earlier. God, she was such an awesome single girl. I needed to find more recruits like her!

I closed my eyes and enjoyed the ride for a little while. But my eyes shot open after an extra hard thrust. His balls bouncing against my clit had nearly sent me over the edge.

"Oh God," I moaned around the new guard's cock.

He hooked his arms under my legs and pulled me off the ground. I shifted forward and the other guard's cock went entirely down my throat. And then the guy behind me thrust and went *so* deep.

Every muscle in my body shook as I orgasmed. If I hadn't been fucking flying between the two cocks I probably would have fallen over.

"Oh shit," said the guy behind me. "I think I just made her come."

"Does that mean it's time to switch?"

I didn't really care what they did. I just wanted more.

They set me down and walked around me. While I waited for them to be inside me again, I caught a glimpse of Slavanka on the screen.

Holy shit, girl!

Slavanka had one guard in a headlock. And then she kicked another one in the face. The third guard tried to punch her, but she did a backflip just in time to get out of the way. The guard's punch connected with his friend rather than Slavanka.

I could practically hear Russian music playing in the background as Slavanka did some sort of spinning move that looked more like dancing than combat. Although the guards probably wouldn't agree, because the spin ended with both of them getting throat punched.

And then the fight was over.

She pulled a whip out of her bodice and tied them all together, and then she finally went over and got ready to put the flash drive into one of the servers.

Which meant Ghostie was about to get access to all the cameras. Including the one focused on me getting railed by two guards.

That was fun, but after the great dick he'd given me this morning, I wanted to do something extra special for him.

"I make mess earlier," I said to the guards. "Now you both make mess on me?"

I didn't wait for them to respond. I just got on my knees and started stroking both of them on either side of my face.

"I'm in," said Ghostie into my earpiece. "Looping footage now."

One by one, the screens blinked and reverted to how they'd looked two hours ago. Before we'd arrived and started sneaking around.

First Esme disappeared from the hallway outside the penthouse. Then the server room feed blinked. The guards who had been tied up just a moment ago suddenly appeared to all be back on patrol.

Just as Ghostie was about to get to the screen showing the command room, I stroked both men a little harder and faster.

I winked to the camera just before the guards exploded all over my face.

The new guard was fairly controlled, hitting me mostly on the cheek. But the first guard really had some pent-up tension. His first shot splashed across my forehead and onto my black wig. The next one was even more forceful, going all the way up onto my little maid hat.

Ghostie growled, and I knew he was enjoying the show.

I smiled nice and big until both men were finished.

Thanks for the skin cream, boys!

It was so tempting to sit there for a while to really let the cum sink into my pores. But for the second time today, I was in too much of a rush for such luxuries.

Such a waste.

But it was a necessary waste. Because there was no longer anything stopping us from saving Ash.

It was finally time to get my girl back!

"Such messy boys," I said with a shake of my head as I wiped the cum off my face.

"You asked for it."

"Yes, yes," I agreed. "Otherwise you ruin floor."

"I would have been happy to cum inside of you."

I gasped and held up my teensy tiny two-carat promise ring from Chad. "I proper maid lady. Not slut."

Both men looked deeply confused. They didn't say another word as I slid back into my maid outfit and headed out to the elevator.

Slavanka was waiting for me there.

"You have cum in hair," she said as we waited for the elevator to come.

I laughed. "I know."

"You fuck guard?"

"Guard*s*," I corrected. "It was my only choice once you decided to go all kung-fu in the server room. Speaking of which…where'd you learn to fight like that?"

"When I seven, foreman at tank factory say I no work. No strong enough." She pinched her bicep and shook her head. "I run home to Papa. Cry. Very sad. Papa teach me throat punch. Next day I go factory. Foreman say, 'Go.' I throat punch and kick in ball. Now foreman cry. I smile. Happy, happy. That start my love of violence."

"You love violence? Do you mean martial arts?"

"Hmmm." Slavanka shook her head. "Violence. Way to make meany man cry like baby."

Interesting.

The elevator dinged open and we rolled our maid carts onto it.

"Everything set at the penthouse?" I asked into the comms.

"Yup," said Ghostie. "Esme has delivered her cart and exited the building. And Ash is... Shit. Wait a second." He went silent.

"Ash is what?" I asked.

No answer.

"Ash is what?!" I yelled.

"We lost Ash," said Ghostie.

Chapter 4

ABORT!
Sunday, Sept 22, 2013

"What do you mean we lost her?" I asked. "Lost her as in…the banana king killed her? He wouldn't do that. He needs her for… Oh God, no. Give it to me straight. Did Ash have a fourth drink and impale herself on the banana king's massive cock?"

"She's alive," said Ghostie. "She just jumped in the pool and shorted out the earbud."

"Dude, don't scare me like that! You just made me have a total Ash moment." Slavanka and I rolled our carts off the elevator onto the 30th floor. "Esme left her bags in room 3023, correct?"

"Affirmative."

We followed the directions on the little gold sign on the wall until we were at the door labeled 3023. The room had been completely gutted, but they hadn't started the remodel yet. Which was why it was a perfect place for Esme to leave the two duffel bags that she'd walked in with.

"Any eyes on the banana king?" I asked as I loaded the bags onto my cart.

"Negative. Although there aren't cameras in every room of the penthouse, so it's possible he's there. Simon is combing the footage from earlier this morning to see if he left.

Wouldn't surprise me if he's going to the airport to greet some big shots flying in for the auction."

"They're gonna be awfully disappointed when they get back and Ash is missing."

"Banana king bad at kidnapping," said Slavanka as she traced her hand over an empty door frame. "Why no molniya on doors?"

"Molniya?" I asked.

"Russian nipple trap."

"Ooh, nipple trap! Does it like…shock them? Or are we talking more of a rough tweaking situation?" Either way, I was intrigued.

"I think she meant *booby* trap," said Ghostie.

"Yes, yes," said Slavanka. "Booby trap. KGB put on important thing. If you steal, thing go boom." She looked so excited by the idea.

"I doubt Ash is going to explode when we rescue her," said Ghostie. "But I have to admit…this mission has seemed pretty easy. Almost too easy. It makes me worry that you guys are walking into a trap."

"We go boom?" asked Slavanka.

"Not like that. But what if the banana king knows you're coming? He might just be waiting for you to come to the penthouse so he can capture you too. And then he'll have three girls to auction instead of just one."

So I might get auctioned tonight?! Score! "You really think that might happen?"

"No. But you should still be extra careful in that penthouse."

"Boo! Don't get me all excited like that for no reason! You know how much I like the idea of my body being auctioned." We wheeled our carts back into the elevator. There was no button for the penthouse, but Ghostie must have done something on his end, because the elevator started going up. And up. And up. Past the top floor available on the buttons.

"Get ready…" said Ghostie.

We both adjusted our tits to make sure they were perfect just before the elevator doors opened to the penthouse.

The ten-foot-tall Bernini statue in the center of the foyer was impressive, but the little penis on it was so sad. The guards standing on either side of it, however, were definitely packing.

And their special forces uniforms made them ten times hotter than the basic ass guards in the command center. Sure, black V-necks and bulging muscles were nice, but these new guards were next level. They were dressed head-to-toe in black, without a single inch of skin showing. Even their faces were covered by matte black hockey masks with mesh over the eye holes. They looked so sexy and menacing. God, I'd let them kidnap me any time they wanted.

But alas…they just stood there, completely motionless. Staring at me and Slavanka from behind their masks.

I couldn't see their eyes, but I knew they were staring at our tits.

Or maybe our legs. Because we looked damned good as we strutted towards the main entrance to the penthouse. I even made sure to knock something off my cart so I'd have to bend over and pick it up.

But they still resisted kidnapping us.

Instead they just opened the door for us and stood aside to let us pass.

We walked in and the guards closed the doors behind us. And still no one popped out to kidnap us.

Damn!

"Alright," I whispered into the comms. "We're in. How do we get to the roof deck?"

Ghostie gave us directions to a secondary elevator that took us up five more floors. But when we got out to the roof deck, no one was there.

"Where is she?" I asked.

"In the pool."

I parked my maid cart by the bar and then walked over to the infinity pool. No sign of Ash. "She's not in there."

"Don't joke like that. This is a serious mission."

"I'm not joking."

"Really?" He sounded so confused.

"Really."

"Well I don't know how that's possible. She was swimming last I saw."

"Crazy Ash hide?" asked Slavanka.

"Maybe," I said. "Let's check behind the bar. And everywhere else up here that a tiny ginger could hide."

We looked all over the roof deck, but Ash was nowhere to be found.

"She's not up here," I said into the comms. "Are you sure you didn't see where she went?"

"I'm looking at the footage now. She was in the pool. And then she wasn't." Ghostie paused for a second. "Shit!"

"What?"

"We fucked with their camera feed and looped an old feed. I think they might be doing the same to us. Abort mission!"

I fixed my hair in my reflection in the pool and then struck a pose on a lounge chair.

"What are you doing?" asked Ghostie. "I said abort! Not lounge."

"But I want to look glamorous when they capture us."

"Damn it, Chastity. Get the hell out of there!"

"Ghostie, I'm not leaving here without Ash. If all three of us get auctioned off…so be it."

I stayed in my pose.

And stayed in it a little longer.

I'd spent hours working on sexy poses, but I'd never practiced holding one for very long. I always just assumed that during a photoshoot the photographer would get so horny from my first pose that he'd just tell me to get on my knees and blow him. And that was a pose that I could keep for hours. #KneesOfSteel.

I eventually ended my pose. "Uh, Ghostie. I don't think any guards are coming for us. We're gonna go look for Ash."

"Okay. But be careful. There could be guards in any of those rooms. Or the banana king himself."

"Boy, you know I can handle the banana king."

Ghostie growled.

Slavanka and I went back inside and started poking around the penthouse. It was all pretty standard penthouse stuff - gourmet kitchen, movie theater, dining room with seating for 24 and an amazing view of the city…

There was a gym, of course. But this one happened to be a boxing gym. Two hunky guards in nothing but shorts were sparring in the ring. One of them looked over at us. And since he was so busy staring at us in our sexy little maid outfits, he had no idea a nasty left hook was headed his way. The punch connected clean with his jaw. Sweat flew everywhere and he stumbled backwards. But he didn't fall over.

Hot damn, boy.

I pushed my boobs together and walked over to the ring.

"Excuse me," I said in my Russian accent. "Where I find bossman and ginger girl?"

The guy who had just gotten hit walked over and leaned on the ropes. "Magnus left to go pick up some VIPs for the auction. And I think the ginger is up on the roof deck. Why?"

"He want us for pre-auction orgy," I lied. That sounded like something the banana king would do, right?

The guard gulped. "Well in that case, you should probably go to the auction room."

"Where I find?"

He gave us directions.

We followed his instructions through a series of hallways and staircases until we found a big wooden door that seemed a little fancier than the rest.

Here we go! I was about to enter the banana king's famed auction room. It was a shame I wasn't being led in here on a leash, but a girl can dream…

I took a deep breath and opened the door.

And it. Was. *Everything.*

I'd expected a dark, sinister looking room. Maybe a circular stage surrounded by tables where prospective buyers could sip scotch and smoke cigars.

But this place was the complete opposite. It actually reminded me a lot of a runway you'd see at Miami Swim Week, but *way* cooler.

There were palm trees everywhere. And sand. And cabanas. And the runway was one of those super awesome ones where they put a sheet of a glass *just* under the surface of a pool so that the models look like they're walking on water.

Oh, and there was also a three-story window with a breathtaking view of the ocean.

I kicked off my heels and dipped my toe onto the runway, but I quickly pulled back as a ten-foot shark swam right at me.

Slavanka hissed at him and he went away. Although I was pretty sure he just turned around because he didn't want to ram his face into the glass.

I had to hand it to the banana king. He had good taste in sex auction décor. Making the girls strut down a runway was a good idea, but making the runway be a shark tank was next level.

I picked my heels up and stepped onto the runway, looking out at the cabanas. It was so easy to picture men sitting there bidding on my body.

"What do you think I would sell for?" I asked Slavanka.

But she didn't answer.

In fact, she was nowhere to be seen.

"Slavanka?"

I checked a few cabanas, but all I found in those were the world's softest mattresses. And lots of handcuffs.

Then I saw something move in one of the glass cubes hanging in front of the window. The frosting on the glass made it nothing but a silhouette, but I could tell it was Slavanka in her maid outfit.

"Slavanka!" I called up to the glass cube.

She pressed her hand against the glass. "I trapped."

What the hell? How had she even gotten up there? I went to the back of the room and found a control panel. The first button started a light show. And some sliders adjusted the light colors. But then I found one that made one of the glass cubes move. I played with a few more until Slavanka's started descending to the ground. The frosting dissipated as it went down, and then a panel slid open so she could step out onto the runway.

"You're free!" I said.

She looked deeply offended. "I not free. My body very expensive."

"No, I didn't mean that you'd be auctioned for free. I meant that you're free from that glass prison. How did you even get up there?"

Slavanka pointed to one of the palm trees.

"For real? You climbed that tree and jumped to the glass cube?"

"Yes, yes. How many ruble you think I sell for?"

"Uh…a million?" *Was that a lot?* I admit, when it came to currency exchanges, I was a bit of a basic bitch. The only rates I followed were the euro, yen, pound sterling, and Swiss franc. Oh, and also the Bhutanese ngultrum. But that's just because I was really hoping they'd mint one with a giant penis on it. #BhutanPenisArt.

"Only one million?" Slavanka sounded so sad.

"That's like 34 grand," whispered Ghostie into my earpiece.

"Sorry, I meant ten million."

"Good, good. I be so sad if sell for only one million again."

"Again?" I asked.

She nodded. "Papa sell me to oligarch for one million. He have tiny penis."

"The oligarch? Or your papa?"

Slavanka looked extremely offended. "Papa have gigantic penis."

"That's what I thought. Just making sure."

"Oligarch have tiny penis. Very sad. But he die from bad borscht."

"Bad borscht? How bad was it?"

"Very bad. Laced with KGB ricin. Fifty-two milligram. Make tiny penis oligarch go bye-bye. Tragic accident." She grabbed the trunk of a palm tree and spun around it in a display of pure glee.

"Did you poison him?"

"Official police record say no."

Damn, girl! She'd totally killed him. That was so bad ass.

Slavanka plopped down on a cabana. "I think you sell for ten million too. Maybe hundred million."

"Can we please stay focused on finding Ash?" asked Ghostie into our earpieces.

"You really think we should?" I asked. "I mean…now that I'm seeing how classy this runway is, I kinda think this is the perfect way for Ash to lose her V-card. I'm tempted to just hide out in one of these cabanas so I can watch it all go down."

"What if tiny penis oligarch buy her?" asked Slavanka.

I stared at her. "I thought you killed him with ricin?"

"I mean *other* tiny penis oligarch."

"Oooh. Yeah, you're right. That would be devastating. Okay, back to the original plan. Let's find Ash!" I grabbed Slavanka's arm and pulled her towards a side exit.

But what I saw on the other side of the door didn't make any sense.

Chapter 5

THE BANANA KING'S SECRETS
Sunday, Sept 22, 2013

What the hell?

I had to do a double take to convince myself that I hadn't just walked through a magical portal and ended up back at the Miami Odegaard boutique. Because this place looked *exactly* like it. Well, almost. The selection here was different. It was exclusively super-sexy swimwear and heels. With diamond-studded gloves. And leashes. Which made sense. Nothing would increase a girl's value more than strutting down that runway in one of these bikinis.

I could have easily spent the rest of the day looking through all the designs. But I couldn't risk letting Ash lose her virginity to a small-dicked oligarch.

I had to find my girl.

So we pressed onward.

The only other exit from the dressing room led to a spa. Four girls were lounging in mud baths.

Ash?!

Maybe...

I honestly couldn't tell. The mud went up to their necks. And their faces were covered with cucumbers and some sort of papery mask. And they all had their hair wrapped up in towels.

I walked over to the pastiest one and tapped her on the shoulder. "Pssst... Ash?"

She turned towards me and reached up to remove the cucumbers from her eyes, but the cuffs on her wrists stopped her before she could reach.

I pulled the cucumbers off for her.

Damn. Not Ash.

"Who are you?" asked the girl at full volume.

"Shhh," I hissed.

She raised an eyebrow.

"I'm here to save you. Actually, I'm here to save my friend. But I guess I'll save you while I'm at it." *Anything to mess with the banana king.*

"From what?"

"The sex auction. That's why you're cuffed, right?"

She nodded.

"Do you think there's a key around here?" I looked over near the door to see if there was a key ring or something. "Actually, don't answer that yet. I'm only going to let you free if you agree to help me find my friend. She's like…the hottest redhead ever. And super neurotic. You might have seen her hiding behind stuff. Or if she's had too much banana juice, you probably saw her on her knees…"

"You actually just missed her. She was getting a massage like two minutes ago. At first she was scared to take her towel off and kept calling the masseur a pervert, but then she just got full nude and started telling him that she was literally in love with him."

"Aw, I love that for her. Did you see where she went?"

"No. Sorry."

"That's okay. I'm sure we'll find her." I turned to Slavanka. "Think you can figure out how to get these cuffs off the girls?"

"Yes, yes. You have pistol and quarter-inch sheet metal?"

"Could you not?" asked the girl.

"Yeah," agreed one of the other girls. "I mean…I obviously don't want you to shoot my arm or whatever crazy shit that Russian girl just said. But even if you had the key, I wouldn't want to go. I've spent so many weekends sitting outside of this resort in a bikini praying that someone would notice me."

"So you're excited to get auctioned?" I asked.

"Hell yeah," said the third girl. "All my friends were so jealous that I got invited. Tonight is gonna be the greatest night ever."

"Right?" I said. "I knew that getting sex auctioned was a good thing!"

"Wait," said the first girl. "You better not be here to steal our spots. If you get one step closer I'm gonna call for the guards."

I held my hands up and backed away. "Whoa, chill. I'm just here to save my friend. But now I'm having serious doubts…"

"Get out of there," said Ghostie. "And stop having doubts. We've been over the many reasons why you need to rescue Ash."

Gah, fine. I pulled Slavanka out of the room and we continued our search.

The next few rooms were…not what I was expecting.

First we came across a storage room stuffed to the brim with banana party paraphernalia. Monkey masks, body suits, refrigerators full of whipped cream… Oh, and *so many* bananas.

I didn't quite understand why the banana king had so much banana party themed stuff. I mean…I was pretty sure he'd just snuck into that banana party dressed like a stripper so he could kidnap me. He'd really gone all out.

The next room helped everything make more sense.

Five nerdy dudes were sitting at very fancy looking computer stations. They even had light up keyboards and those transparent computer towers where you can see all the stuff inside.

I dusted next to one of them to see what they were working on.

I was hoping this was the security center for the banana king's penthouse. That would probably give me eyes on Ash.

But instead the dude was just watching porn. And not in a normal way. He kept rewinding and zooming up and stuff.

Wait a second!

He wasn't watching porn. He was *editing* porn. Banana party porn, to be precise.

I ran into the hallway and made sure no one could hear me. "Ghostie! You'll never believe what I just found."

"Ash?"

"No, silly. I found out how the banana king was able to infiltrate that banana party so easily. It's because he owns it. In fact, I think he invented it." The Locatellis must have done some clever accounting to hide their ownership. Because I'd researched the company extensively and never found a link.

"Banana king invent banana party?" asked Slavanka. "He genius."

"Right? I mean…I obviously love his sculpted abs and his humungous cock. But now I'm kind of loving his brain too."

"He probably just bought it from someone," said Ghostie. "Or paid someone to come up with it."

"Maybe. But his sex auction runway combo is also the work of a sexual genius. That makes me think he came up with both. And now I'm kind of thinking that we should just do whatever it takes to get captured so we can see what he has planned for the auction tonight. I'm 100% sure it won't be some basic ass auction with a fast-talking dude and numbered paddles. Unless the paddles are intended for sportive ass smacking."

"He's your enemy," growled Ghostie. "The right-hand-man of your dad's archnemesis."

"Oh my God." I put my hand to my chest. "Are you all thinking what I'm thinking?"

"Probably not."

"Yes, yes," said Slavanka. "Banana king is to sexual innovation what Comrade Lenin was to economic and political reform."

"That is definitely not what I was thinking, but I like that energy."

"What you think then?" asked Slavanka.

"I was thinking that the banana king and I are a modern-day version of Romeo and Juliet. But like…way hotter." I was trying to work through the entire comparison in my head when the door at the end of the hall caught my eye. *Magnus King* was etched into a gold name plate. "Oooh," I said. "I think I just found the banana king's office. I bet he locked Ash up in there after she got all horny for that masseur."

"Worth a try," said Ghostie. "But be careful."

"I'm always careful," I said as I opened the office door and strolled in.

"Painting of you?" asked Slavanka, pointing to a painting front and center on the wall right behind the banana king's desk.

I honestly couldn't tell. His office was so damned big that the painting was at least a good 30 feet away from us. But as I got closer, I realized Slavanka was correct. It was an oil painting of me at the banana party bent over between the banana king and the Italian stallion. The artist had perfectly captured the raw sexuality of it.

"It's amazing," I said. "I wonder who the artist is." I got closer and looked for a signature. I was half expecting it to say Michelangelo. Or da Vinci. But that wouldn't make any sense, because both those dudes had been dead for centuries. This was signed… *Magnus King.* "Oh my God. He's a painter too! See, Ghostie? I told you he was creative."

"He create this too?" asked Slavanka.

I walked over to the scale model she was inspecting. It was an entire community of Italian villas. The label indicated that it was going to be located somewhere in Italy. I was a city girl and never pictured myself living in a neighborhood. But if I ever changed my mind, that was the neighborhood I would want to live in. With a few adjustments, of course.

Like…why did he make all the villas separate? More space between villas meant you were less likely to get caught getting railed on your wrought iron balcony. And it would make swinging unnecessarily cumbersome. No one wants to go to a key party and then have to drive 20 minutes home before you can start having fun with your hot random neighbor.

The banana king may have been a creative genius, but he still wasn't on my level.

I grabbed the stack of papers next to the model to get all the deets.

"Yikes," I said after reading only about three of the papers.

"What?" asked Ghostie.

"I know why the Locatellis are trying so hard to kidnap me. Those idiots went all in on this neighborhood before they had all the permits locked down. And now their creditors are getting impatient. They could be bankrupt by the end of the year."

"Scan those documents so I can check them out later. But for now, you need to get back to the roof deck. I'm pretty sure Ash is back. But she's not alone."

Chapter 6

CABANA BANANA

Sunday, Sept 22, 2013

I burst out onto the roof deck.

"Ash!?" I yelled.

She popped her out of from behind a cabana curtain. "Chastity!"

"Ash!" I yelled again. I ran over and hugged her.

"I'm so glad you finally made it. I felt so bad that I was getting to have all the fun without you. This resort is freaking amazing." She took a sip of banana juice and then cocked her head to the side and looked back and forth between me and Slavanka. "Why are you both dressed like maids?"

"You're gonna want to sit down for this," I said. Because there was no way she remembered our earlier conversation.

"Okay… You're kind of freaking me out." Ash slowly sat back on her cabana bed but seemed super nervous to hear what I had to say.

"So don't freak out, but…you've been kidnapped."

Her eyes got huge. "What?!"

"I said don't freak out!"

She started breathing so fast. And then she started laughing like a crazy person.

I put my hand on her shoulder. "Ash, take a deep breath. It's gonna be okay."

"Ash finally lose mind," said Slavanka. "Very sad. We take behind bar and shoot. End misery."

"What?" said Ash. "Don't shoot me! I'm just messing with you guys. I know I've been kidnapped. But like…you were right, Chastity. Being kidnapped is the best. I've been getting pampered for 24 hours straight. I even have my own personal cabana boy. He gets me anything I need. Like an endless supply of banana juice. And free massages. He even built this cabana to shield me from the sun!"

Ah…that explains where this cabana came from. I'd been wondering how it randomly appeared during the small amount of time we were searching the penthouse for Ash.

"Wait," I said. "So you're…totally fine?"

"Yup."

"Do you know what's happening tonight?"

"Sure do! The banana king is inviting the world's most handsome, powerful men to come bid on me. And the winner is going to take my virginity. I'm so excited. But kind of nervous. No…just excited! God, I bet he's going to be so handsome. And forceful yet gentle. And then we're going to have the most magical lives traveling all over the world." She gazed wistfully out at the ocean. "Oh my God. I just got the best idea. You two should auction your bodies too! Maybe best friends will buy us. Or brothers!"

"Handsome powerful man buy you *and* brothers?" asked Slavanka. "He like penis?"

I laughed. "I think she meant that brothers will buy us."

"Oh. I like other better. Three penis better than one."

"Yeah they are!" I gave her a high five.

"I wouldn't know," said Ash. "Since I'm a virgin and all… But not for long!" She took a huge sip and finished her banana juice. "Oh my God. Where are my manners? I need to get you guys drinks. And bikinis. Those maid outfits look uncomfortable. Speaking of which…did you ever say why you were wearing them?"

"They're part of the rescue mission. We had to wear them to sneak past security."

"You should have just called the banana king and asked if you could come be auctioned too. He's actually a really chill dude. But kinda bad at ping-pong. I whooped his ass like 10 games in a row. But now that I think about it, he might have just been distracted by my tits. I think one flew out during the third volley and I didn't realize it until the end."

"Speaking of boobs flying out…I really need to get out of this outfit. This collar is going to give me a horrible tan line." I unclasped the little white collar and then shrugged out of the top. The outfit pooled at my feet.

"Oh my God," said Ash. "You're so naked. Cabana Boy could be anywhere."

"Well I don't have a bikini with me. What else am I supposed to do?"

"Here. You can have mine." Ash undid her bikini top and slid out of her bottoms and then handed both to me.

I raised an eyebrow. "You do know that *you're* naked now, right?"

"Huh?" asked Ash. She looked down and seemed surprised. "Oh, right. That makes sense. That's fine, though. Cabana Boy has already seen my tits. But he's a licensed masseur, so it's fine. He's basically a doctor."

"In that case, I don't need clothes either." I handed the bikini to Slavanka, but she just tossed it aside and got naked too.

I lay back on the cabana next to Ash to start getting my tan on, but there was absolutely no sun hitting me. The curtains on this thing were so thick.

"Let's move to those chairs," I said, pointing over toward the pool.

Ash shook her head. "I can't. The sun is not my friend. Especially now that my naughty bits are exposed. As the old saying goes – the only thing that burns faster than a ginger's nips is peanut brittle in a cast iron skillet."

"Then get your cabana boy to bring you more sunscreen. And more banana juice." If she was gonna make it all the way to the virgin auction tonight without having a freak out, that banana juice needed to keep flowing. I reached up and rang the bell.

A cabana boy in red swim trunks walked out onto the roof deck almost immediately.

"How may I help…" His voice caught in his throat when he rounded the corner and saw the three of us lounging nude on the cabana. He blinked a few times and regained his composure. "Apologies. I didn't realize Ash had company coming. Is there anything I can get for you ladies?"

"Three banana juices, please," said Ash.

Wow. She really was plastered if she was the one ordering for us. Usually she would hide in the bathroom until the meals arrived to avoid having an awkward encounter with a server.

"Of course," said the cabana boy. "And I found something you might like." He pulled a bottle of SPF 200 out of his back pocket.

"SPF 200?!" screamed Ash. "I didn't even know that was a thing! You're amazing." She jumped up and gave him a big naked hug.

"Anything to make you happy. Would you like me to apply it?"

"Uh, is that even a question? Of course I want you to. But do it like that massage earlier."

"Of course." He led her over to one of the lounge chairs and started lathering her up. He seemed to be paying particular attention to her boobs. But maybe that was by request due to that whole ginger nips and peanut brittle adage.

"What the hell are you three doing?" asked Ghostie through my earpiece as Slavanka and I plopped down on lounge chairs next to Ash.

"Sunbathing," I said.

The cabana boy looked over at me.

I pointed to my earpiece. "Phone call."

He nodded and went back to rubbing lotion on Ash.

"I can see that you're sunbathing," said Ghostie. "I was more curious about why you were doing that instead of executing phase 3 of the rescue plan."

"Because the plan is off. Ash wants to get auctioned."

"And what about you and Slavanka? You're just gonna let the banana king capture you?"

"Yup."

"What if you get bought by a small dicked oligarch?"

"That wouldn't be ideal, obvs. But I know you'll be waiting to give me a proper pounding when I get back."

"Fuck this," growled Ghostie. "I'm out."

I laughed. "What do you mean you're out?"

But there was no answer.

"Ghostie?"

Still nothing. Just faint static.

"Where Ghostie go?" asked Slavanka.

I shrugged. "He's probably masturbating to the footage of me in the command center earlier. He's lucky that the mission ended early so he didn't have to deal with that pent up frustration all day long."

Slavanka nodded. And then I rolled over so I could tan my ass. Getting to watch the cabana boy's abs while he lathered up Ash was an added bonus.

But I only got to watch for a second before he stood up and wiped his hands on a towel.

"Sorry for the delay, ladies. Three banana juices coming right up!" He hurried over to the bar and started pouring drinks.

"He seems nice," I said. "But he's kind of awful at applying sunscreen." He'd hardly rubbed any of it in. Ash was a big, white blob.

"I beg to differ. This is the best application anyone has ever done. Most idiots rub it in. But it doesn't work once it disappears." She gazed over at him and let out a satisfied sigh. "I think I'm in love."

"Are you now?" I asked. I wasn't sure if this was a true love situation or if Ash was just on phase 3 of her banana juice drunkenness where she loves everything.

Ash nodded. "Yup. He just understands me. I hope whatever hunky billionaire buys my virginity tonight is as amazing as my cabana boy."

"Maybe you should just give it to him."

Ash's eyes got big. "I couldn't. That would be totally inappropriate. He's basically my doctor."

"Single Girl Rule #33: If a man applies sunscreen properly and builds you a cabana, you should consider letting him take your V-card."

"Is that for real?" asked Ash.

Not even a little bit. "Girl, would I misquote the Single Girl Rules?" Under any other circumstance, I wouldn't dare. But this was important. I knew Ash wanted her first time to be magical. So if I had to misquote the Single Girl Rules to make that happen, then so be it.

"Wow. It's so oddly specific to this exact moment. But I can't argue with the logic of it." She glanced over at the cabana boy as he shook up our drinks. "Is this really happening? Am I about to have sex?"

I nodded.

Ash's eyes got big. But not in her usual I'm-terrified-and-about-to-do-something-really-fucking-weird sort of way. This was just sheer excitement. "So how is this gonna go down? Should I just order him to ravish my body? I mean, he is my cabana boy, sworn to serve my every whim."

"That could be hot, yeah. But let's put a pin in that. The rule didn't say you *had to* let him take your V-card. It just said you had to consider it. Which makes sense, because we don't have a few key facts yet."

"Your drinks, ladies," said the cabana boy. He set a tray down on a little table next to us and handed us each a banana juice.

"Thanks, pal," said Ash. She reached up and punched his arm.

Oh no. She's being weird.

"Anything else I can get for any of you?"

"I actually have a few questions," I said.

"Ask my anything."

The most important thing was the size of his cock. But the Single Girl Rules required I check a few other things first. "How old are you?"

"Twenty-two."

Excellent. Over 18. "Are you a virgin?"

He laughed. "I am not."

"Grower or shower?"

"Grower." He gave me a weird look. Like he didn't understand my line of questioning.

Interesting. "How big?"

"Flaccid or erect?"

"Erect, of course."

"Eight inches. Eight and a half if I'm really horny."

I smiled up at him. "Prove it."

"Of course, miss." He dropped his shorts and his erection sprung free. It was indeed just a tick over eight inches. And pretty thick. But it had a nice taper to it, so the top was a little thinner. That would be perfect to help Ash ease into it without tearing her in two. It was pretty much the perfect starter dick.

"Very nice. Would you like to fuck Ash?"

His cock grew a little. "I'm actually under strict orders not to fuck her."

"That's not what I asked. I asked if you want to bury your cock in her tight little virgin pussy."

"Of course, but…"

"It'll be our little secret. Your boss will never know."

He gulped and his eyes landed on Ash. "Fuck it. I'll do it."

I smiled up at him. "Good. But before you do, I need to make sure that you know what you're doing. So here's what's gonna happen. If you can make me come before Slavanka gets you, then Ash's virginity is yours. Deal?"

"Gets me?" he asked.

Slavanka walked over to him and started sucking his cock.

"Holy shit. Wow. Okay." He cracked his knuckles and stretched his arms and then lifted me straight out of my lounge chair and onto his face.

I moaned a little as his tongue danced around my clit.

Oh God yes. I hadn't been expecting that. Yes, he was muscular. But it was nice lean muscle rather than pure beef.

He grabbed my ass and pushed me closer to his face so that his tongue could go all the way in me.

I grabbed his hair to make sure he didn't go anywhere.

Despite my best efforts, his tongue still left me. But it was immediately replaced by two fingers.

I tried to steady my breathing. But each pump of his fingers got me closer. And his tongue against my clit was everything.

And then I was gone.

"Fuuuuck," I moaned.

He sucked up some of my juices and then set me back down on the lounge chair.

Slavanka looked back at me. "I lose?"

I nodded. "Yeah. But it's not your fault. I'm sure your blowjob was outstanding. I just came super fast. But in my defense, the vibrating jet ski combined with the thought of getting auctioned off tonight already had me pretty damned close to the edge. Cabana Boy just nudged me over the finish line."

He gave me a cocky smile. "If you say so."

I rolled my eyes. "Fine. It was pretty great. If you're half as good with your cock as you are with your mouth, then Ash is in for a treat."

He turned to Ash and nudged her knees apart. Then he traced his fingers down her thighs.

She shifted in the chair. But she didn't freak out.

And she still didn't freak out when he slid a finger inside of her. Then he added a second.

Good boy. He was doing a great job warming her up.

"Cabana Boy," said Ash. But it came out all airy.

"Can I get you something, miss?"

"I want your cock."

"Of course." He pulled his fingers out of her and rubbed her wetness onto his cock. And then he spread her legs even further.

Ash let out a deep breath. She still wasn't freaking out. But I could tell she was super nervous.

He tapped his cock against her clit a few times.

This is it! Ash was going to lose her virginity. I was so freaking excited for her!

He grabbed his shaft and was about to start fucking her when she squirmed away.

"Wait!" she yelled. "Don't you need a condom?"

"Girl, no," I said. "You're on birth control." I turned to him. "You're clean, right?"

He nodded.

"Then you don't need one. Condoms are for lame boyfriends. Not studs like Cabana Boy."

She bit her lip. "That's so naughty."

"I won't cum in you if that makes you more comfortable."

"Good," said Ash. And then she whispered, "I love when guys cum on my face."

Cabana Boy stiffened even more. I was pretty sure he was nearly 9 inches now. "I thought you said you're a virgin?"

"She is," I said. "But girl loves sucking cock. You should have seen her at the banana party last weekend."

"Banana parties are the best," she said. "And next time I can have even more fun now that I won't be a stupid virgin. Speaking of which…let's do this."

She spread her legs and Cabana Boy got ready to fuck her.

"Wait!" yelled Ash again. "Is it gonna hurt? I think I need something to bite down on. Like you see in those old war movies when they put a belt in the dude's mouth so he doesn't bite his tongue off from the pain of having his leg amputated. Can you find me something, Cabana Boy?"

"Absolutely. One second." He ran inside. And then he returned with two other cabana boys. They got on either side of Ash and dropped their trunks.

Neither was erect yet. But it only took a few seconds to fix that.

And *fucking wow.*

They were both in the double digits.

"For us?" asked Slavanka.

"No," said Cabana Boy. "They're for Ash." He turned to her. "That's what you were hinting at, right? That you wanted a cock to suck while I fuck you?"

"It was not, no. I was legit just asking for a sexy strip of leather to bite."

"Oh."

"But I like your idea better." She looked up at the two guys. "So which of you wants to be my sexy strip of leather?"

"Uh…" said one of them. "Does it have to include the biting?"

"I can't make any promises about what my mouth will do when he enters me. If it hurts, I might not be able to control my jaw."

"Here's what we're gonna do," I said. "Ash is gonna grab your cocks while Cabana Boy takes her virginity. And then once he finishes, you boys can double team the hell out of her."

"Ohhh!" said Ash. "Great idea! Okay, let's do this thing." She spread her legs and grabbed both cocks in a death grip. She could barely wrap her hands all the way around them, but she was squeezing so hard that the heads started to turn purple. "Now give me that cabana banana."

Chapter 7

THE GREAT ESCAPE
Sunday, Sept 22, 2013

Cabana Boy was about a millimeter away from deflowering Ash when the taser hit him. His whole body seized up and he would have fallen right on top of me if I hadn't rolled off the lounge chair.

The two guys on either side of Ash got hit a second later.

"Ow!" yelped Ash, pulling her hands away from the now-electric cocks.

What the fuck is happening?

"Fall back to bar!" yelled Slavanka. She grabbed Ash and pulled her behind the bar. I was only a few steps behind. A taser probe whizzed right in front of my face. And then another just missed my arm.

Shit!

I was still a few steps away. And out of the corner of my eye I could see one of the banana king's guards aiming his taser rifle at me. I was about to get lit up by like 30 taser probes.

I dove behind the bar just as he unleashed a full volley at me. Most hit the bar. One landed in the pool and lit the entire thing up like a Christmas tree. And one hit my heel.

Not my actual heel. My shoe heel. Which was good. Because I'd been prepared for that shit. After I'd tased the banana king during our last encounter, I figured he'd be eager to do the same to me. So I'd told Justin to construct all my shoes for this mission using nonconductive materials. And he was awesome, so he'd actually listened.

"What the fuck is happening?!" screamed Ash. "We're all gonna die!" Apparently getting shot at had nullified all the hard work that banana juice had been putting in to calm her crazy ass down.

I peered around the bar.

The banana king and six of his elite guards – the ones with the sexy masks – all had their rifles pointed at us.

"You're trapped," he yelled. "Surrender now and I'll only raise the ransom by $5 million."

"Interesting offer," I yelled back. "But Daddy doesn't pay ransom."

"Then I guess I'll have to auction you and your virgin bestie to the highest bidder."

"No!" screamed Ash. "I can't be auctioned. You know I don't do stages!"

"This one is more of a runway situation…" I said.

But the look on her face made it clear she was *not* interested.

"Ash," yelled the banana king. "Can you hear me?"

"Yes!" she yelled back.

"Good. If you come out now, you don't have to walk the runway tonight. I'll just use a picture of you."

I could tell Ash was strongly considering it.

"But if you try to run, then you're going to walk that runway ass naked. And the highest bidder is going to fuck you in front of everyone."

"Nope. Nope, nope, nope." Ash shook her head. "Okay!" she yelled. "I'm coming out. Don't shoot!" She put her hands up and slowly started to stand.

"No!" I hissed and pulled her back down.

"What do you mean no? That's a good deal! We're pinned down here with no hope of getting out. You can't bring a bottle of banana juice to a taser fight."

"Sure you can. In fact, the Single Girl Rules almost demand it. Rule #5: Have banana juice in your purse at all times."

"I thought that rule was about wine?"

"Slavanka," I said. "Could the original Rule #5 have been interpreted as banana juice rather than wine?"

She nodded. "Yes, yes."

"Then I'm making an official alteration to the English translation of the Single Girl Rules."

"I don't care if the Single Girl Rules say wine or banana juice. How could either one of those things help us against seven men armed with tasers?"

"Molotov cocktail," said Slavanka. She held up a bottle of banana juice with a soaked rag coming out the top. Her other hand was wrapped around a lighter and her thumb looked awfully eager to light it.

"She's not wrong," I said. "But let's not burn the building down just yet."

"Final chance!" yelled the banana king. "Come on out, Ash."

Ash sighed. "I really think we should surrender."

"But I have a plan. Please trust me?"

"Okay. But if this plan doesn't work and I get fucked on that runway…"

"Not gonna happen. Unless you want it to." I winked at her. "Ash isn't coming out," I yelled to the banana king. "But I have a counter proposal."

"I'm listening," he called back.

"If you let us go now, we can pretend like this never happened."

"And if I don't?"

"Then you and your guards are going to chase us around this resort for a while. And then when I feel like it, we're going to walk right out the front door. And I'm gonna make sure Luigi Locatelli knows how badly you fucked up."

The banana king laughed. "There's no way you're gonna walk out my front door."

"You think?"

"I'm certain of it."

"Then let's make a deal. If we walk out, then you'll owe me a favor."

"I'm not gonna give a mobster's daughter a blank check."

"What does it matter? You're so confident you have us trapped. Why not make the bet? Tell you what — I'll even limit the favor so that it doesn't involve money. And if you catch us, then you can auction all three of us. You can even livestream the entire thing. Turn it into the pay-per-view event of the year."

"What?" gasped Ash. "No! I won't agree to that."

"Ash would never agree to that," yelled the banana king.

I looked at Ash. "I love how you two are so on the same page. So cute. I'd be shipping you two so hard right now if his cock wouldn't literally destroy your delicate virgin pussy."

"We're not a cute item," said Ash. "We're both just sensible adults."

"Who want to fuck each other?"

"No!"

"Okay, okay. Whatever you say."

"Am I correct that Ash refuses to agree?" called the banana king.

"You are. But technically she already did. Those release forms we signed last weekend for the banana party cover anything you film until next Friday."

"What?" gasped Ash. "No! Don't tell him that!"

"Shit, you're right," said the banana king. "Okay, you have a deal. And since I'm such a nice guy, I'll even give you a ten second head start."

"Aw, thanks!" I scooted over to my maid cart and grabbed a duffel bag. Then I pulled out three assault rifles.

"Ten! Nine! Eight!" called the banana king.

I tossed one to Ash.

"Ah!" she screamed. "Don't give that to me! I'm too clumsy for guns."

"It easy," said Slavanka. She grabbed the gun from Ash, disengaged the safety, and checked the chamber. Then she handed it back to Ash. "Point at bad man and fire. It fun."

She grabbed another rifle from me and did the same routine.

"I can't do this," said Ash.

"That's fine," I said. "You're gonna look so hot getting auctioned on that livestream tonight."

Ash grabbed a bottle of banana juice and downed the entire thing. "Time to die, fuckers!"

Just as the banana king reached one on the count, Ash jumped up on the bar and started shooting. Slavanka also started shooting, but from a much more tactically sound position.

Ash jumped back down. In the process, she managed to lose control of her gun, juggle it, and chuck it on the ground.

"That was awesome!" she yelled. "We just took down all of them!"

"For real?" I asked.

"Yes! Wait a second." Ash's eyes got huge. "Did I just kill seven men?"

"I shoot six," said Slavanka.

"Oh God. I'm a murderer!"

"Girl, chill. They'll be fine."

"How?! I didn't just graze them. I was aiming right for their livers."

"Livers? Why? Actually, it doesn't matter. Those weren't bullets. They were darts."

"Tranquilizers?" asked Ash.

"Not quite…"

"Dude, what the hell?" yelled one of the guards. "Why are you tenting your pants right now? Are you one of those freaks who gets hard when you're in danger?"

"Fuck off," said another guard. "Did you see the tits on that ginger? And anyway, you're hard too."

"Huh?" said the first. Or at least, I thought it was the first. They all had voice modulators that made it hard to tell who was talking. "Wait, what the hell?"

"What did that girl shoot us with?" yelled another.

I peered over the bar and took in the mayhem. All the guards were looking down at their rock-hard dicks tenting their pants.

"Guards all gay?" asked Slavanka.

"Nah," I said. "Those darts were filled with liquified boner pills. The formulation and rapid delivery dart system were my entry into my 10th grade science fair. It got disqualified for being inappropriate, but then the CIA offered to buy it for ten million dollars. So that felt like a win."

"What is your life?" asked Ash.

"Amazing. Just like these outfits for phase 3 of the plan." I pulled three leather catsuits out of the duffel bag. "Let's take turns shooting at the guards while we change. And then it's time for the great escape."

Ash stared at me. "Great escape?"

"It's probably better if I don't tell you until it's time. Just put that on."

The guards eventually regained their composure and got ready to storm our little hideout behind the bar, but then I told them that a double dose of Viagra might make their dicks explode. After that, they wisely holed up behind various pieces of furniture while the banana king yelled at them for being a bunch of pussies.

The only thing wrong with my plan was that there was no mirror behind this bar, because I desperately wanted to see how hot I looked in this catsuit.

"I'm confused," said Ash. "Why are the tops of my boots different heights?"

"Uh…it's kind of the latest trend." *How does she not know that?*

"And what exactly are these outfits supposed to be?" She adjusted her cat mask and then grabbed the ass-length red braid attached to it. "Are we getting ready to steal fine art from the Met? Or are we about to be dominated at a weird leather sex party?"

"Neither." I pulled the final items out of my duffel bag – three spools of rope, each 700 feet long.

I tied the end of each to the bar and then rolled the spools towards the edge of the roof deck.

"Please tell me we're not about to do what I think we're about to do."

"That depends," I said. "Do you think we're about to rappel down the side of this building?"

"Yes."

"Then you're correct." I tossed them each some specially designed clips.

"Holy shit," said Ash. "You're serious?"

"Yeah. I know you're probably afraid of heights, but…"

"Why would I be afraid of heights?"

"Wait, are you not?"

"Not really. Are you?"

"No..." *What the hell?* Was Ash seriously not scared of heights? She was legit scared of everything. Maybe the banana juice was starting to work its magic again?

"Great. Then let's get the hell off this roof before the banana king makes me walk that runway ass naked." She stood up, shot a few warning darts at the guards, and then made a run for the edge of the roof.

Slavanka and I were right behind her.

Running top speed towards the edge of a skyscraper was way scarier than I expected. But seeing Ash charge ahead somehow made me keep going. If she could do it, then I certainly could.

"What do we do when we get to the edge?!" yelled Ash.

"I don't know!"

"What?! How do you not know!? This was your plan!"

"Just keep running!"

I held my breath as I got to the edge of the roof. But I kept my legs moving. And in a second I was running down the side of the building like I was in a James Bond movie.

"Ahhh!" yelled Ash. "This is freaking awesome!"

It really was. This was like…the coolest thing I'd ever done. Except getting double teamed. That was definitely better. So I guess this was the second coolest thing.

I didn't understand how the clips worked, but Ghostie had promised that they'd keep us from going splat. And he was right. If we went too fast or started to fall forward, the clips tightened up and kept it from happening. They were almost as good as my boner dart invention.

Speaking of Ghostie…

"Ghostie!" I yelled into my earpiece. "It worked!"

No answer.

"Ghostie?" Was he still masturbating? That maid outfit must have really done something to him. I'd have to get another one and surprise him with it some time.

"Chastity?" said a voice in my earpiece. But it wasn't Ghostie.

"Teddybear?" I asked. "Where's Ghostie?"

"No idea. He just stormed off and said something about being done with your shit. I've been trying to figure out these comms ever since."

"So he's not masturbating?"

"No. I mean…I'm not really sure. I don't have eyes on him, so I can't definitively say that he's *not* masturbating. But I wasn't getting a masturbatory vibe from him. He seemed pretty pissed."

"Pissed? At me?" *Why? I'd put on such a good show for him.*

"Yup. Anyway…there's something a bit more pressing that we should probably discuss. Have you looked down?"

"Not recently." My legs had gotten a little tired from all that running so I'd spun around into a more traditional rappelling stance.

"Well, you might wanna do that."

I stopped rappelling and looked down.

There were at least a dozen guards standing right at the bottom of our rope.

Chapter 8

PENISES ARE AFOOT
Sunday, Sept 22, 2013

"Oh no," I said. "Whatever will we do?"

"Why do you not sound concerned?" asked Teddybear.

"Because, silly. This is part of the plan!"

"How is getting caught part of the plan?"

I sighed. "I went over this last night at Odegaard. Were you not paying attention?"

"I was trying to! But you kept giving me handjobs under the table."

"Oh, right. What floor do you think I'm at?"

He started talking, but something in the window distracted me.

"Chastity?" he asked. "You still there?"

"What? Yeah, sorry. I just thought I saw some girl with *amazing* tits through the window. But it was just my reflection. What were you saying?"

"I think you're on the 23rd floor."

"You think? Or you're sure? This is important."

"I'm sure. I counted twice while you were checking yourself out."

"Good boy." I loosened my grip on the rope and rappelled down three more floors. Then I clicked my Odegaards together and put my heels in the center of the window.

"Chastity!" screamed Ash. "Watch out! That window is cracking!" She kicked off the window and swung to the left a little.

"Yeah it is! But not fast enough. These heels are supposed to be vibrating at the perfect frequency to *shatter* glass. Not just crack it." I glanced down at the guards waiting for us below. "And if we can't shatter this window, then we're fucked. Or at least, we will be. In front of a huge audience." I winked at her.

"Then do something to shatter it!"

"I'm trying." I adjusted to get my heels flatter. The cracks spread a little. But it still didn't shatter. "Hmmm…"

"Alright girls, on the count of three, let's all kick off the window. And then come in hot with your heels pointed right at a crack. Three, two, one…"

We all kicked off. And swung back *way* father than I'd expected to.

"Ahhhh!" screamed Ash. "We're all gonna die!"

I whipped my head back and let my braid catch in the breeze. "I thought you weren't afraid of heights?"

"I wasn't!"

We reached the apex of our swing and started going back towards the building, picking up speed as we went.

"What happen if window no shatter?" asked Slavanka.

"Hmm…hadn't thought of that."

"We go splat?"

"Probably."

"What?!" screamed Ash.

"Heels out!" I yelled as we swung towards the window.

We all kicked our feet out and covered our eyes.

And it worked! The glass shattered into a million pieces and we flew into a hotel room. Slavanka grabbed onto a desk to stop her momentum. I grabbed the minifridge. And Ash grabbed…

"AHHHHH!" screamed a woman.

No, not just any woman. A petite naked woman. Who was riding her boyfriend cowgirl style.

Or at least…she had been before Ash grabbed her. And I don't mean Ash casually grabbed her arm. I mean she full-on bear hugged her and tugged her clean off the dude's dick. Ash's momentum carried them both into the wall. And then they bounced off and swung back out through the window.

Both of them were screaming hysterically.

"Let go of me!" screamed the woman.

"Why are you naked?!" screamed Ash.

I ran to the window. "No!" I yelled to Ash. "Do not let go of her! She's not clipped on like you are!"

They both screamed even louder.

And the screaming didn't stop until they swung back through the window.

I grabbed Ash's arm while Slavanka grabbed the girl.

Ash stared at the girl in horror. "So sorry for the interruption. Please continue."

When the girl didn't move, Ash scooped her up like a baby and placed her back on top of the guy's dick. "There you go." She patted them each on the head, curtsied, and then backed away.

How the hell did Ash just lift that girl? Did banana juice give her super-human strength?

I'd dive into that later, but for now, we had to get out of here. The guards on the ground would have seen what we did. They were probably already on their way up here.

I glanced at the phone to see what room we were in and then I ushered Ash and Slavanka into the bathroom.

In less than two minutes we'd unscrewed the air vent, climbed in, and pulled it back into place.

"Where we go now?" asked Slavanka.

"We need to navigate to the bachelorette suite." I pulled a blueprint out of my pocket and rolled it out in the duct. "We're here," I said, pointing to room 2004. "And we need to get here." I dragged my finger all the way over to the bachelorette suite on the other side of the building.

And then we got to crawling.

Even with my knees of steel, I would have thought that this journey would be tough on them. But there was some sort of padding in these suits. It felt like I was crawling on one of those $100,000 space-age memory foam mattresses Daddy had just installed in his flagship hotel.

"Did you tell Justin to put padding in the knees, Slavanka?" I asked

"No, no. We only talk about Stalinkini."

"Then how'd he know we'd be crawling?" And then my mouth dropped. "That naughty boy must have thought we'd need built-in kneepads for all the blowjobs we'd be giving!" Which was actually a pretty astute assumption. But oddly enough, these catsuits were the only outfits I'd ordered that I *didn't* expect to be giving any blowjobs in. They were strictly for rappelling and crawling.

Lame, I know. But luckily this phase was just about over.

I peered through the vent to make sure none of the bridesmaids were in the bathroom, and then kicked the vent out of the way.

We all crawled out onto the vanity. I was happy to see that all the outfits I'd laid out for them were gone. The only thing that remained of my gift was the fake note from the bride's future husband.

"Alright, girls," I said as I retrieved the duffel bag that I'd stashed under the vanity. "Welcome to phase 4 of the plan."

"Which is…?" asked Ash.

"The best phase."

"Or maybe the second best. Phase 5 is gonna be pretty epic too." I unzipped the duffel bag and pulled out three black monokinis and matching pairs of Odegaards.

Ash held one of the monokinis up and looked at the big bold letters across the front. "Bride squad? Chastity, this is no time for a bachelorette party! The guards are going to be searching every room on this floor. We've gotta make a run for it before it's too late!"

"This is actually the perfect time for a bachelorette party. Where else could three girls as sexy as us blend in perfectly?"

"But they've seen our faces."

"Briefly, yes. But Teddybear is gonna take care of that."

"I am?" he asked into my earpiece.

"Yes."

"How exactly?"

"See the picture on the desktop titled *Three Hot Randos?*"

"Uhh…"

Through my earpiece I could hear Teddybear clicking around.

"Is it the pic of the blonde, brunette, and redhead? That look *kinda* like you guys?"

"That's the one."

"Got it."

"The banana king will have uploaded a picture of our actual faces to his database. You need to go in and replace it with that fake. And make sure you change the file name before you do."

"And where exactly can I find that database?"

"No idea. That's Ghostie's job."

"But he isn't here."

"Hmm…yeah. If you're already struggling, then that's gonna be an issue for phase 5. Can you tell Ghostie to please hurry up and finish masturbating? We need him!"

"I really don't think he's masturbating."

"Oh right. You said he was pissed about something? Whatever could he be upset about? The plan is going swimmingly." I turned to my girls and pointed to the mono-kinis. "Put those on," I mouthed. I started changing too.

"If I had to guess, I think he's getting a little jealous."

"Jealous? But I let him fuck me just a few hours ago. And I put on such a good show for him in that command room. He must be SO excited to fuck me again."

"I know. He's just…he's more sensitive than he lets on. I've never seen him as happy as he was after he fucked you on the yacht this morning. I think he was secretly hoping that he'd properly satisfied you."

"Of course he satisfied me. If he hadn't, then I totes would have gone into the locker room to search for Tonguenado the second I stepped foot in this building." *Speaking of which…where is that mythical beast of a man?* I'd be devastated if this mission concluded before I got to see what he could do with his tongue. As soon as Teddybear had told me the rumors about him, I knew today had to involve me riding Tonguenado's face.

"Maybe he just realized that he'll never satisfy you the way I do," said Teddybear.

Were Ghostie and Teddybear in a secret competition to see who could satisfy me best? I loved that for me. "Speaking of satisfying me…" I pulled the straps of my bride squad monokini over my shoulders and turned to look in the mirror. "It's a shame there aren't any cameras in this bachelorette suite. Because you'd definitely want to satisfy me if you saw what I'm wearing right now."

"Describe it to me." Teddybear's voice had gone down an octave.

"There's a scoop neck that shows off lots of cleavage. And I just pulled the sides up to make the thong ride up my ass the way you love. But you wanna know the best part?"

"Mhm."

"It has BRIDE SQUAD written across the front in big bold letters. So every guy I encounter will know that it's my job to suck as many cocks as possible."

Ash looked down in horror. "Is that what this means?" She tried to cover the words with her arms.

Teddybear gulped. I bet I'd just given him the biggest boner.

"Wanna see a picture?" I asked.

"Yes."

"Okay. I'll take one for you. But only once you get Ghostie to come back."

"I really don't think he's gonna come back."

"Ghostie wouldn't dare abandon me. He must be up to something…" I thought back to what had happened just before he left.

I'd told Ghostie the plan was off. Then he asked what would happen if I got auctioned off to a small dicked oligarch. And then I'd told Ghostie that it was okay because at least he'd be waiting to properly satisfy me afterwards.

That's it! "I know what he's up to."

"You do?"

"Yup. He's working on infiltrating the auction. That way he can buy us if it looks like some small dicked oligarch is winning the bid. But I'd rather him just come back and help us escape. I really wanna win that favor from the banana king." I could think of so many things I'd make that man do…

"I'll send Simon to try to find him."

"Good." I put a few finishing touches on my makeup and then turned to my girls. They looked smoking hot in their bride squad outfits. Although Ash would look even better if she'd put the heels on. "Ready to party?"

"As in…play boardgames with a fun but sophisticated group of women?" asked Ash.

"Did you learn nothing at the banana party last weekend?"

"What banana party?"

I stared at her. Every time I'd brought it up this week, she always just pretended like she didn't know what I was talking about. Except when she'd had banana juice. Then she was more than happy to talk about all the naughty things she'd done.

"Please tell me you didn't hire any strippers for this poor bride."

"I didn't."

"You promise?"

I pulled a stack of Single Girl Rules membership cards out of the duffel bag and put my hand on them. "I solemnly swear that I didn't hire any strippers for this party."

Ash looked at the cards and then back at me. "I don't think you'd desecrate the Single Girl Rules like that, so I guess I believe you. But I'm still suspicious."

I shrugged. "I really didn't."

"So it's seriously just going to be women doing non-sexy bachelorette things?"

"Sure…"

"That was not convincing."

I winked at her.

"No! Stop that. I know what that wink means."

"Do you?"

"Yes! It means penises are afoot."

"Penises on feet?" asked Slavanka. "That sound not sexy."

"No," I said. "Penises are *afoot*. As in…happening or about to happen."

Ash groaned. "I knew it."

I smiled and pulled the bathroom door open.

It was time to party!

Chapter 9

TWINSIES!
Sunday, Sept 22, 2013

"Hello, ladies!" I yelled as I strutted into the party.

All thirteen girls looked up at me.

"Who are you?" asked the bride.

"And why are you three dressed like us?" added the maid of honor in her fancy Spanish accent.

"I'm your bachelorette party MC," I said. "And these are my lovely assistants. And we're wearing these outfits courtesy of the bride's loving fiancé. It's all part of the platinum party package that he purchased last night. And let me be the first to say – you ladies all look stunning. Your fiancé has great taste."

The bride looked down at her white monokini. The neckline went all the way down to her bellybutton. "I still can't believe he picked these out. He'd usually kill me if I ever left the house dressed like this."

"Why would he not want you to dress like that?" I asked. "You look hella hot."

"He gets jealous easily. He didn't even want me to have a bachelorette party. He only agreed once he found out Autumn was planning it." She pointed to the redhead in the matron of honor monokini.

"And I dare say I'm doing an excellent job," said the redhead. "Now…who's up for another exciting game of Trivial Pursuit?"

A few of the girls groaned.

"Not again," mumbled one of them.

I stared in horror as Ash ran over and plopped down by the coffee table. She looked so excited to play.

Trivial Pursuit? At a bachelorette party? "What's the twist?" I asked. "Take a shot every time you get an answer wrong?"

"I wish," said one of the girls. "But Autumn promised the groom that she wouldn't allow any drinking."

"So there's no alcohol here? Not even mimosas?"

"Nope," said the bride. She sounded so sad.

No alcohol?! Dear Lord. "Well luckily for you, I brought some banana juice."

"Banana juice?" asked the redhead. "That sounds delicious."

"It is. You're gonna love it." I ran back to the bathroom with Ash and Slavanka and emptied the duffel bag. Some multicolored gel bracelets fell out, along with a few other things I needed. At the last minute I'd remembered Single Girl Rule #5: Have wine in your purse at all times. But Ash preferred banana juice to wine, so I'd brought six bottles of that instead. And the duffel bag was basically a giant purse.

"Heads up," said Teddybear into my earpiece. "Guards just started searching every room on your floor. They'll be to yours soon."

"Any luck on getting that picture uploaded?" I asked.

"Working on it."

I took a deep breath. The riskiest part of my plan was coming up. And we were woefully unprepared. Teddybear needed to get that picture uploaded. And I needed to get these girls in the mood to party. If the guards showed up before both those things happened, we'd surely be caught.

Which was fine, I guess. The auction still sounded super fun…

But now it felt personal between me and the banana king. I was determined to walk out the front door of the hotel right under his nose.

I tossed two bottles to each of my girls. "Let's get this party started! Oh, and when we introduce ourselves, remember to give fake names." I grabbed the other two bottles and headed back to the party.

"Alright, ladies!" I said. "Gather round." I shoved Trivial Pursuit off the coffee table and replaced it with a tray of banana juice shots.

All the bridesmaids came over and formed a big circle. Half of us were on the couch, some of us were on chairs, and a few unlucky girls got stuck on the floor.

"In order for me to do my job, I need to get to know all of you. I wanna know your name, your relation to the bride, your number, and a never-have-I-ever style fact about yourself. I'll go first." I grabbed a shot glass and stood up. "I'm Charlotte. I'm the bride's official bachelorette party MC. I've been with nine guys. And…" I looked around at the bridesmaids to see what would give me some helpful info. "Never have I ever been married."

Autumn was the only girl to take a shot. That meant she was the only one who was married. Which made sense, because she was the *matron* of honor.

I sat down and Slavanka stood up.

"I Svetlana…"

Nice fake name!

"I Russian. Suck lots of men." She sat down and looked very pleased with her answers.

"Does that mean we have to drink if we aren't Russian?" asked one of the bridesmaids.

"Yup!" I said.

Every girl took a shot.

Well that worked out well. A few more rounds like that and these girls would be so drunk.

Ash looked around nervously. Slavanka had just gotten up to pour everyone more shots, so Ash was now next to me. Which meant she was next to introduce herself. All eyes were on her.

"Do I have to go?" she whispered in my ear. "Everyone is staring at me. I think they're onto us…"

Oh no. Ash was in her paranoia stage of banana juice drunkenness. "Just go," I whispered back.

"I'm Ash…" she said in the quietest voice.

No! Don't give your real name. I kicked her foot.

Her eyes got huge and she added, "…niqua."

"Your name is Ashniqua?" asked the one black bridesmaid.

Ash nodded. "Yup. Sure is. Ashniqua Williams III."

"What is your pasty ass doing with a name like Ashniqua Williams III?"

Ash shifted uncomfortably and bumped into me a little. I'd never felt someone so sweaty in my life.

"It's an old family name," I said, trying to cover for her.

The bridesmaid pursed her lips in the sassiest way.

"Please continue, Ashniqua," I said.

"Right. Where was I?"

"Just do a never have I ever."

"Okay. Um… Never have I ever had a basic ass white girl name."

About 90% of the bridesmaids drank. Including Ash.

The black girl looked at her suspiciously. I thought she was gonna call her out, but luckily the bride stood up to go.

"I'm Chloe," she said. "I'm the bride, obvs. I've been with 7 guys. I…"

"Liar," said one girl, trying to mask it as a cough.

"Fine. I've been with…" She started counting on her hand. And then the other hand. And then back to her first hand. "Fourteen guys."

A few of the girls gasped.

Hot damn, girl! Fourteen guys in one weekend? Chloe was a freaking legend.

She gave a nervous laugh. "If any of you tell Jason that, you're dead."

"Our lips are sealed," said the maid of honor.

"And never have I ever…touched two dicks at once."

I drank. But everyone was more focused on the matron of honor. She'd just taken a drink and her face was now completely red from embarrassment.

"Damn it, Chloe," she said. "You're taking that way out of context and you know it! Technically I did that once, yes. But it was only because I tripped and fell and tried to catch myself."

"Mhm," said Chloe. "Suuuure."

"It was! Also, I pass. Next."

"Nope," said Chloe. "You're up next. You have to go."

"Gah. Fine." The redhead started talking as quickly as possible. "I'm Autumn, I'm Chloe's sister and matron of honor, I've been with one guy, and never have I ever had red hair."

Everyone stared at her.

"What?" she asked.

"Do you not know how this game works?" asked Chloe. "You're supposed to say something that you've never done. And then anyone who has must drink. So you just got yourself."

Autumn turned even redder and took another sip of banana juice. And then she tried to disappear into the couch cushions.

She'd been with one guy this weekend? For real? She seemed almost as timid as Ash. But then again...when Ash got going on banana juice, she needed all the dicks. This girl must have been the same.

The girl next to her stood up and started talking in her fancy Spanish accent. "I'm Sloane. I met Chloe freshman year of college, and now I'm her maid of honor. I've been with 18 guys. And never have I ever been a commoner."

Everyone except for me drank.

Sloane looked at me. "You are royalty as well?"

"I mean...look at me. Also, can I just say how impressed I am with how many dicks you ladies have sucked this weekend?" I turned to Chloe. "Fourteen? You must have had one hell of a Saturday!"

Chloe laughed. "Wait, what?"

"You said your number was 14."

"Right..."

"So you've sucked 14 dicks this weekend."

She put her hand over her mouth. "Oh my God, no. I thought you meant our number for our entire lives."

"Oh. Well then what's your number for this weekend?"

"Zero."

I blinked at her. "Zero? As in...none?" I was so confused.

"Yup."

"My number for the weekend is also zero," whispered Autumn.

"Whoa whoa whoa. Have any of you sucked any dicks this weekend?"

"Yes, yes," said Slavanka.

All the other girls shook their heads.

"Wow, okay," I said. "You girls are lucky I'm here. I think there's still time to get this bachelorette party back on track, but we need to hurry." I pulled a stack of Single Girl

Rules membership cards out of my monokini and handed them to the bride. "Pass these around."

"What are they?" asked the bride.

"The most important thing you're ever going to read. In particular, I'd like to bring your attention to Rules 10, 39, 40, and 41. Especially you, Sloane."

"What did I do?" asked Sloane.

"It's more about what you *didn't* do. Rule #39: Being a maid of honor is the most sacred duty in a woman's life. And Rule #10: All celebrations of important life events must involve strippers."

She stared at me.

"Did you hire strippers?" I asked.

"I did, actually. But Autumn made me cancel them."

I turned to Autumn. "Are you trying to ruin the wedding?"

"Huh?" she asked.

"Rule #41: Any girl who doesn't suck a cock at the bachelorette party is uninvited to the wedding. This includes the bride. No exceptions."

She gave a nervous laugh. "But I'm married. And almost all of the other girls here have boyfriends."

"Rule #40: At a bachelorette party, every girl is single again."

"These can't be real rules."

God, she sounds exactly like Ash.

And then I realized something crazy.

Oh my God! "Ashniqua, Svetlana. Come with me." I stood up and waved them into the bathroom.

"Slavanka," I said. "Are you a Russian princess?"

"No, no. Why you ask?"

"Because! Those girls are older versions of us. Chloe the blonde bride. Autumn the timid ginger. And Sloane the raven-haired European princess. Their names even start with the same letters as ours!"

"Okay, there are a few similarities," said Ash. "But there are more differences. I mean…I've never even had a boyfriend. There's no way I'm gonna be the first one of us to get married."

"Not according to the universe."

"And Slavanka just said she's not a princess," added Ash.

"*Yet*," I corrected. "Not a princess *yet*. A lot can happen in the next ten years."

Ash didn't look convinced. "So you think you're gonna end up marrying some lame dude who won't let you show off your cleavage?"

I shuddered at the thought. "Chad does get pretty jealous. And he's extremely lame. And possibly racist." *Is the bride's fiancé racist? I hate that for her.* "And he may have already tried to propose once." I held up my tiny little two-carat ring. And then I realized exactly what was happening. "Wait! Girls! Single Girl Rule #19: Never wear the same dress as a friend, unless you're attempting the sexy twins gambit."

"Oh God," said Ash. "We're literally wearing the same thing as them. And they are objectively sexy. And basically our twins. Are we…are we living in Single Girl Rule #19 right now?"

"Yes!" I screamed. "I've always known the Single Girl Rules were magical. And now they're giving us a glimpse at what our lives could be like in ten years."

"Do you think it's set in stone?" asked Ash. "Because my twin seems like a great gal. I mean…she had the good sense to bring Trivial Pursuit to the party. And she was the only girl who ditched the heels and covered her ass with a sarong. Very classy."

"No, no," said Slavanka.

"Right?" I said. "That sarong sucked. We need to get that girl in her proper bride squad outfit ASAP."

Slavanka nodded. "Yes, yes. Sarong dumb. But I not mean that. Future no set in stone. Sexy twins are us if never find Single Girl Rules."

"Oh damn," I said. "You're right! The universe must have brought us here to save them!"

"This is freaking me out," said Ash. "Sexy twins don't happen by coincidence." She frantically looked around the room and then lowered her voice to a whisper. "I think the banana king set this up. He's watching us. Toying with us. Like he's a lion and we're a herd of helpless antelope. Any minute now he's going to spring his trap…"

"I mean, yes, he is definitely hunting us."

"Speaking of which," said Teddybear into our earpieces. "Guards incoming. ETA thirty seconds."

"Is the replacement photo uploaded?" I asked.

"Not yet."

Shit. "Okay. I'll just have to work my magic." I adjusted my tits and pulled my thong up even higher. Then I turned to my girls. "Ready for the fun to begin?"

"Absolutely not," said Ash. "But I'd be down for some Trivial Pursuit."

"We're not playing that. Also, why are you in the shower?"

"I'm hiding," she whispered.

"It's a glass shower. I can see you perfectly." Frosted glass would have been one thing, but this was just fully transparent.

She pretended not to hear me.

I opened the shower door and tossed her heels in. "Put those on. We have to blend in!" And then I headed to the door.

The guards had arrived.

Chapter 10
THE GAME PACKAGE
Sunday, Sept 22, 2013

I opened the door and stared up at the six hunky guards. Their faces were hidden by their masks, but based on how much they were all tenting their pants, I was pretty sure they were the six guards we'd just had a shootout with on the roof. *Thank you, boner pill darts.*

"Good morning, officers," I said. "Is there a problem?"

"We aren't officers," said one of them.

"I know that," I whispered. "But we're paying you to play the part." We weren't. They had no idea what was happening. But I was going to act like I thought they were strippers. I grabbed one of their vests and pulled him into the bachelorette suite.

"Who is it?" called Chloe from the other room.

"A police officer," I yelled back. And then I winked at the guard.

"What does he want?" she asked.

"We're looking for some girls," he called back.

"Some *bad* girls," I corrected. And then I dropped my voice to a whisper. "Where have you been?"

"Uh…" He looked back to the biggest guard for guidance.

"Come on!" I whispered to him. "They said you'd be here an hour ago. This striptease better be worth the wait.

Now get in there!" I grabbed two of them and pulled them down the hall into the main room.

All the girls cheered. Except Autumn, who screamed and hid behind a lamp.

"So you said you were looking for some naughty girls?" I asked.

"We are," replied the biggest guard. "A blonde, a redhead, and a brunette."

"Hmmm…" I tapped my finger to my lips. "Well the bride is blonde. And the maid of honor is brunette. And the matron of honor is a ginger."

"We'll need to speak to all three of them."

Chloe and Sloane were quick to jump off the couch and walk up to the guards. But Autumn tried to stay hidden. The other bridesmaids had to grab her and drag her over to the big guard.

"Did we do something wrong, officer?" asked Chloe.

"Call me Sarge." He pointed to the chevrons on his sleeve. "And I'm not sure if you did something wrong. That's what I plan to find out." He pulled out his phone and started hitting buttons.

This was it. The moment of truth. If Teddybear had replaced the picture, we'd be fine. But if he hadn't…then they'd pretty quickly recognize me as one of their three targets.

Sarge cocked his head to the side and stared at his phone. Or was he staring at me?

Shit!

I turned to the bar and started pouring shots so that he couldn't see my face.

"That's weird," said Sarge. He turned to the other guards. "The picture was in the daily mission briefing folder, right?"

They nodded.

"Well it's not there anymore. Did any of you get a good enough look at the girls to be able to ID them?"

"Rookie claims to have a photographic memory," replied one of the guards. They all looked at the skinniest guard.

He nodded.

"So can you ID them if you see them again?" asked Sarge.

"Well…I only got a good look at the redhead," said Rookie. And if I'm being honest, I was kind of focused on her tits."

"So you need to see her tits to recognize her?"

"Yeah. Her nipples are so light. And they're the perfect size. And…"

"We get the point, Rookie," said Sarge. "Keep it in your pants." He turned to the three girls. "Take your clothes off. We need to see your tits."

Autumn's eyes got huge. She wrapped her arms around herself and shook her head. "No way, pervert."

"It's not a perverted thing. I'm just doing my job."

"So you *don't* want to see our tits?" asked Chloe. She sounded kind of offended.

"I do. But I'm not asking to see them for my pleasure."

One of the guards in the back nudged another in the ribs and whispered, "Wanna bet which one is gonna slap Sarge first?"

Sarge spun around. "Do you have a better idea, Poker?"

Poker shrugged, and when he did, his sleeves slid up a bit to expose his muscular tattooed forearms. His black skin made it a little hard to make out what the tattoos were, but I was pretty sure they were of playing cards. Which made sense given that his nickname was Poker.

"Did you check your trash folder?" asked Poker. "Rookie has a tendency to randomly delete stuff."

"That was one time," protested Rookie.

Sarge pulled out his phone again.

"Shit," said Teddybear in my earpiece. "The upload was getting blocked by a firewall so I just deleted the pic. But I don't have access to the trash folder on his phone. Can you distract them?"

Boy, of course I can distract them.

I cleared my throat. "A word, please?" I gestured for the guards to follow me back to the bathroom.

"What is it?" demanded Sarge.

"What are you guys doing?" I whispered. "This might be a confusing concept, but since you're the strippers, *you're* the ones who are supposed to be getting naked."

"We're not on stripper duty today," said Sarge. "We're on a top priority mission straight from the boss. Who the hell are you, by the way?"

"I just stared working at the concierge desk. My job is to make sure high-vale guests have the time of their lives. So today I'm the MC of this bachelorette party."

"I don't really care what your job is. *My* job is to find a blonde, brunette, and redhead. And in order to do that, we need to see their tits. So step aside."

"Okay," I said. "But I doubt Magnus will be very happy when the bride's daddy calls and complains that some perverted guards crashed her bachelorette party and demanded she get naked."

"Well do you have a better idea?"

"Actually, I do. This is a bachelorette party. And the girls all think you're strippers. So just play the part. The girls will all be naked in no time."

Sarge shook his head. "There's no time for that. This is urgent."

"Come on, Sarge," said Poker. "It's a good plan." He turned to me. "What package did they buy? Please tell me they ordered the game package."

"That's never gonna happen, Poker," replied Sarge. "No one in their right mind would pay $200,000 for strippers."

Game package? $200,000 strippers? I very much liked the sound of all of that.

"Actually," I said. "They did order the game package. Like I said…this is a super high value client."

"Hot damn!" said Poker. "I knew someone would get it!" He rubbed his hands together and then started pulling stacks of cards and notes out of all his pockets. "Any requests for what game we start with?"

"You're in charge," I said. I absolutely could not wait to see what games he was gonna throw at us. "But I do have one request."

"Anything."

I grabbed the stack of gel bracelets off the counter and separated them by color. "Take a color," I said. "And whenever a girl blows you, take one off and give it to her."

"Why?" asked Sarge.

"Come on, Sarge," said Poker. He grabbed the stack of yellow bracelets off the counter. "Have some imagination. First, there are a ton of games we can add these to. Second, if we see a girl with no bracelets, we'll know to give her some extra attention. And finally…I bet a lot of the girls are gonna want to collect a full set."

"And they'll let us know if any girls need to get uninvited from the wedding," I added.

The guards all looked at me.

"You know the rule. Any girl who doesn't suck a cock at the bachelorette party is uninvited to the wedding. This includes the bride. No exceptions."

"Don't you worry," said Poker. "By the time my games are over, every girl at this party will have a bracelet. Including you."

"Oh is that so?" I asked.

He nodded.

Yeah, okay. He was right — I was definitely gonna blow at least one of them. But the real question was…how would our sexy twins react?

I had a feeling that my twin and Slavanka's twin would get on their knees as soon as the dicks came out. But Ash's twin? I doubted she would give in to the temptation as easily. She'd be more likely to jump out a window than suck off a stripper in front of all her friends. Unless banana juice worked the same on her as it did on Ash. But really…what were the odds of that?

Now that I thought about it, this was perfect. Autumn was never gonna take her monokini off. Hell, I doubted she'd even take off the sarong covering up her thong. Rookie would never get a chance to see her nipples to tell if they were like the picture in his head. Which meant I had plenty of time to enjoy myself while we waited for Ghostie to come back to help us execute phase 5 of the escape plan.

God, I couldn't wait to see the devastated look on the banana king's face when we walked out the front door.

But until then…

"You really think you're gonna get me on my knees?" I asked. "I'm working, sir. And what would my fiancé think?" I held up my sad little diamond ring.

"Better not show Bandit that," said Poker. "He has a thing for girls with boyfriends."

"Damn, girl," said the guard who'd just grabbed the orange bracelets. "That's quite a ring. It's gonna look great in a picture of your hand wrapped around my big black cock."

Another black guard? Score! After getting a taste of Hakeem's big black cock earlier at the goddess contest, I was seriously craving more.

"Bandit also has a thing for taking pictures," added Poker.

"Poker," barked Sarge. "Enough. I'll let you play your games." He turned to Bandit. "And I'll let you take your pictures. But the primary objective here is to see every bridesmaid's tits so we can get a positive or negative ID and move on."

"And that's exactly what I'm trying to do," said Bandit. He turned to me with his hockey mask. "Show us your tits and I'll let you suck my cock. Or better yet, how about I fuck you against that mirror? It'll make for a great photo. You can show it to your boyfriend when he asks how your day was."

"Hmmm…" I said. "So you want me to bend over like this?" I bent over and arched my back, bracing my hands against the mirror. I splayed my fingers to really show off my ring.

"Mhm," he said, but it came out as more of a groan.

"Well that would be very inappropriate." I stood up and walked over to the door. "See you boys out there." I blew them a kiss and walked out.

"Ashniqua," I called across the room and nodded my head towards one of the bedrooms.

She and Autumn walked over.

"Hey," said Ash. "We have a surprise for you."

"You do?"

"Mhm," they both said in unison.

"Those officers were being awfully inappropriate," said Ash. "So we made you a sarong." She held up a torn-up T-shirt. "I know, it's not as nice as Autumn's or mine." She pointed to their midsections. Ash now had a sheer black sarong just like Autumn's. "But it'll at least cover your ass."

"We're gonna make one for all the girls in case those perverts come back," added Autumn.

Oh God, why?! One Ash was a lot to deal with, but now there were two of them. And I needed to get Ash alone so I could darken up her nipples with some makeup before the guards started stripping. I wasn't fooled for one second by her innocent, sarong-wearing act. She'd tear her clothes off so fast the second she downed a couple more banana juices. And then they'd recognize her nips. And then my escape plan would be ruined.

"Can I talk to you alone for a second?" I asked.

"There's no time," said Ash. "We need to start our twelve-round tournament of Trivial Pursuit *now*."

She was right about there being no time. The strippers would be coming out any second and...

The lights dimmed and music started blaring.

Chapter 11

PIN THE TAIL ON THE BRIDESMAID
Sunday, Sept 22, 2013

The bathroom door swung open and Poker ran out. He was completely naked except for his mask, his combat boots, and a white washcloth draped over his erection.

Oh hell yes.

"Ladies," yelled Poker. His voice sounded the same as all the other strippers thanks to the voice modulators in their masks. But I knew it was him from the royal flush tattooed on his arm and the yellow bracelets on his wrist. "Let's try this again. I'm looking for three very naughty girls. Has anyone seen them?"

"There!" yelled some of the girls, pointing to Chloe. A few other girls pointed at Sloane. And the rest pointed to Autumn.

Autumn looked around for some furniture to hide behind, but there was nothing suitable near us. "I haven't been naughty," she said. "If anything, you're being naughty, because you seem to have lost your pants, sir."

"Do you like what you see?" asked Poker, thrusting his hips to make his cock bounce up and down. The washcloth slid a little lower with each thrust. But his cock was so big that the cloth still had plenty of length to cling to.

Autumn ran away and hid behind the couch.

"Playing hard to get, huh? Guess I better call for back-up." Poker whistled and the bathroom door swung open again.

The other five guards all came running out. Just like Poker, they were dressed only in masks, boots, and wash-cloths. And they all had 8 abs and at least 8 inches. There was one more black guard, so that must have been Bandit. And then the beefiest one was definitely Sarge. And the skinny one was Rookie. The other two were a beautiful mystery. One was heavily tattooed – definitely a bad boy. But the last one may have been my favorite, because his cock was so big that the washcloth was struggling to cover it.

Although…I was really craving some black cock. So maybe Poker and Bandit were actually my favorites. *Gah! So hard to choose!*

"Spread out, boys," said Poker. "We need to canvas the entire room. I'm certain our three naughty girls are here."

"Oh no," whispered Ash. "They're onto us!"

"Shhh," I hissed back. "They're not talking about us. It's just part of the act."

"Are you sure? He literally just said he was certain we were here."

"What are you two whispering about?" demanded Sarge.

Ash screamed and ran to go hide with Autumn, leaving me alone staring up at over 200 pounds of pure, delicious beef.

"Nothing, sir," I said.

"It didn't look like nothing. I'm gonna have to ask you to come with me." Sarge picked me up and slung me over his shoulder, giving me a lovely view of his muscular ass.

Poker grabbed three chairs and put them all in a row. Sarge put me in one. They put the black bridesmaid in another. And they put Chloe the bride in the middle.

"What are your names?" demanded Sarge.

"Charlotte," I said, using my fake name.

"Chloe," said the bride.

"Indigo," added the black bridesmaid.

Sarge took a beat to let our names hang in the air. "And where were each of you this morning?"

"Don't answer that, girls," I said. "Until we have a lawyer, our lips are sealed."

"Your lips are sealed, are they?" asked Sarge. "Well luckily for me, I think I have just the thing to *unseal* them. Snake, they're all yours." He snapped and motioned to the guard with the humungous cock. It was a fitting nickname for a man who looked like he had a literal snake in his pants. Or under his washcloth, in this case.

"Ladies," said Snake as he danced over to us. "Is Sarge giving you trouble?"

We nodded.

"Ignore him. He likes to try to trick people. See…he claims he's looking for naughty girls. But really he's looking for a virgin. So if you want to clear your name…"

Snake put his hand on the back of my chair and thrust at my face.

God, his penis was magnificent. The washcloth just barely hung over his tip. He wasn't *quite* a foot long. But he was damn close.

"Just say the word and I'll move this cloth," he said. "And you can prove your naughtiness."

I was about to give in. But then I realized his game. The banana king knew I loved huge cocks. And he'd probably told Snake. That sneaky bastard was trying to trick me! Sarge wasn't the tricky one, Snake was!

Maybe he wasn't nicknamed Snake because of his giant penis after all. Maybe he got the nickname from his stupid lying mouth.

But his cock was soooo big…

I was about to give in when he moved to Indigo.

"Are you a virgin?" he asked.

She shook her head.

"Prove it."

He thrust at her so hard that the washcloth went airborne. But it landed back on his cock, albeit a few inches lower than before. A few thick veins on his shaft were now visible.

Lord, give me strength.

Indigo just gave him a sassy look and shoved his abs. To the untrained eye it would have looked like she wasn't interested. But I knew that she was just playing hard to get. And pushing him away was a perfect excuse for her to touch Snake's beautiful abs.

He moved on the Chloe.

"You're the bride-to-be, huh?" he asked.

Chloe nodded.

"And does your husband think he's marrying a virgin?"

She shook her head.

"Then it won't matter if you have one last fling before your big day. What do you ladies think, should she open her mouth for me?"

"Yeah!" yelled the girls.

"I couldn't hear you." He put his hand to his masked ear. "Should she open her mouth?"

"Yeah!" all the bridesmaids screamed louder. Except for Autumn. She'd screamed, "No!"

Snake froze. "Did you boys hear that?"

"I did," said Bandit. "That ginger doesn't want the bride to be a little slut. Which means we've probably found our virgin."

"I'm not a virgin," said Autumn. "Look at my outfit."

"And what exactly are you hoping to prove with your sarong and bare feet?" asked Bandit. "Every other girl in here is showing their ass and rocking 6-inch heels. You sure look like a virgin to me."

"I meant *this*," said Autumn, pointing to the words MATRON-OF-HONOR on her monokini. "And for your information, I'm not the only girl wearing a fashionable sarong." She pointed to Ash.

Oh shit!

Ash ducked behind the TV.

Bandit ignored Ash and danced over towards Autumn. "Matron-of-honor, huh?" he asked. "So you're married?"

"I am. So I'm definitely not a virgin."

"Does your husband know you love big black cocks?"

"No," said Autumn. "I mean yes. I mean no!"

"So he does or he doesn't know?"

"He doesn't know. Because I don't love big black cocks."

"Oh really?" Bandit tore the washcloth off his cock, and it was magnificent.

Autumn's eyes got huge. "Oh my God," she gasped.

As she said it, Bandit snapped a polaroid of her. He shook the photo and then showed it to Autumn. "You sure look excited in this photo."

"I was shocked. Not excited. Give me that!"

He thrust towards her.

"Ah!" She jumped away from him. "Not your cock! The photo."

"As you wish," he said and slipped the photo into her cleavage.

Autumn pushed him away and adjusted the top of her monokini to cover herself a bit more. "This is ridiculous. I'm calling the front desk."

No way, girl. Stealing these guards' uniforms was a critical part of our escape plan. So if they stopped stripping, the plan would be ruined. I poked Poker in the arm. "Now would be a good time for a sexy game," I said.

"Strip poker?"

I shook my head. "Lame. How about pin the tail on the bridesmaid?"

"Damn, I like the way you think." He ran off to the bathroom.

I grabbed two shots of banana juice and met Autumn at the room phone. I hit the button to end her call.

She glared at me. "What the hell? Your strippers are out of control."

"I'm so sorry," I said. "I'll make sure they tone things down. Just please don't call the front desk. If I get one more complaint I might get fired. Drink?" I held up one of the shots of banana juice. I hoped she'd react to them the same way Ash did.

She took the shot and downed it. "God that's good," she said and grabbed the other from me. She downed that too.

"Ladies," yelled Poker. "Who's ready to play pin the tail on the bridesmaid?" He held up a handful of blindfolds.

Most of the girls cheered. Except Autumn. She was still eyeing the phone like she wanted to call and report me and my strippers to the front desk.

"Good idea to linger by the phone," I said. "That way it'll be nice and easy for a hunky stripper to find you even once they have their blindfolds on." I gave her a wink and ran back over to the guards.

They all took their masks off. And then me and a few of the other girls tied the blindfolds tight over their eyes.

"Better take your boots off too," I said.

"Huh?" asked Sarge. "Why?"

Because me and my girls are going to put your uniforms on for the final part of our escape, and it would kind of blow our cover if we didn't have the boots. "Because Autumn is barefoot. Can you imagine the horrible reviews we'd get if one of you crushed the matron-of-honor's toes right before the wedding?"

The guards took their boots off and then stood up.

"Okay," said Poker. Now that he had his mask off I could hear his real voice. And damn was it sexy. "The game is simple. You all have ten seconds to hide before we come looking for you. And if we catch you…well, you know what happens."

Hell yeah I do. "Before we start," I said. "Let's check to make sure these blindfolds are working." I pulled the top of my monokini down to flash the guards. None of them reacted. "Okay, looks like you're all set."

"Ten, nine, eight…" started Poker.

All the girls started running around and hiding behind furniture. The guards all moved their heads to try to track the sound of heels, but there were so many girls running in so many directions that I doubted the noises would be much help to the guards.

"Seven, six, five, four…"

I looked around for Ash, but she must have already hidden behind something. So instead I ran over and poured some more shots. Autumn grabbed one from me and then hid under the bar.

"Three, two, one… Here we come!" yelled Poker. In unison the boys all tore the washcloths off their cocks and tossed them to the side. One landed on the maid of honor, but she stayed perfectly still.

Fuck yes. Their cocks were even better in all their naked glory. Especially Snake. God, that thing was huge.

I was a little devastated when he turned and walked in the opposite direction of the bar.

It served him right when he walked right into an end table. None of the other guards were faring any better. They were all hitting walls and tripping over furniture.

"Fuck," muttered Rookie as he collided with Sarge. They both turned and accidentally had a little sword fight.

Ash giggled and then immediately clasped her hand over her mouth.

There you are! She'd expertly hidden behind a neon orange sign that said "POOL". *Is there a private pool connected to this room?* If so, I definitely needed to check that out. But first I had to save Ash. Because I wasn't the only one who had heard her giggles.

Bandit, Poker, and Snake had all turned towards her and were closing in fast.

"Ah!" she screamed and jumped over a chair, narrowly avoiding Poker's groping hands.

The tattooed guard turned and started coming for her too. She was close to being surrounded.

"Toro! Toro!" yelled the maid of honor, waving the washcloth that had landed on her head earlier.

The guards turned to her and charged. She kept waving the washcloth until the last moment, and then, like an expert bullfighter, she pulled back and let Snake charge right through the washcloth.

There were a few other close calls, but no girls had gotten caught yet. But the more they moved, the more their heels clicking on the floor gave away their positions.

"Stop it!" hissed Chloe as Sloane tried to push her in front of Poker.

Poker reached out for them, but Chloe dodged at the very last second. His hands landed right on Sloane's tits. She smiled up at him, spun around, and then started grinding on his thick cock.

Lucky girl.

I thought about jumping in front of Bandit, but I had work to do. I waved at Ash and Slavanka and motioned for them to meet me at the bathroom door. Sarge must have heard their heels, because he came for the door too. But my girls got there *just* quick enough. We closed the door and locked it just as Sarge arrived. He was so big that I was a little worried he might just burst right through the door, but somehow it survived.

"Isn't it cheating to be hiding in here?" asked Ash.

"No," I said. "And that doesn't matter, because…"

"I think it is. We should probably go back out there." Ash reached for the doorknob.

I swatted her hand away from the door. "Girl, chill. Are you trying to get caught or something?"

"NO!" said Ash, way too defensively.

"Oh my God. You totally are!"

"Yes, yes," agreed Slavanka. "Ash have five shots of banana juice."

On top of what she'd already been drinking? Wow. If I didn't get her out of this party now, she was going to go buck wild. "So which guard do you want to blow?" I asked.

"None of them," said Ash.

"Let me guess… Rookie?"

"Nope," said Ash.

"Aha! So you *do* want to blow one of them."

"No I don't," said Ash. But the way her face was turning bright red totally gave her away.

"She want black cock," said Slavanka. "Remember how she suck the banana bro at banana party?"

"Uh, of course I remember that. She took that cumshot like a pro." I turned to Ash. "So which of the black guys are you gonna suck first tonight?"

"Neither."

"Yeah, I guess you're right. Because sadly we have to leave this magnificent party early." I pressed on my earpiece. "Teddybear, is Ghostie back yet?"

"Negative," he replied. "But I just heard from Simon and he says he has a lead. So hopefully we'll have him back soon."

"Good, because we're just about ready to go to the final phase of the escape plan." I picked up one of the guards' uniforms and held it up to Slavanka. It definitely looked big, but it should be passable. "Try this on," I said and tossed it to her. "Ash, try to find a uniform that fits."

She picked up the biggest one and held it up. "How's this?"

"Ash, I'm pretty sure that uniform was made for a 6'5 beefcake. You're a 5 foot nothing twig."

"I'm not a twig!" She jiggled her tits.

"You're right. You have lovely tits. But you're still nowhere near as big as Sarge." I assumed that was who the giant uniform belonged to.

Ash picked up another. "Is this a better fit?" she asked.

"No but..." My eyes gravitated to the name on the badge and my jaw dropped. "Holy shit. Are you girls seeing what I'm seeing?"

"Uh...no?" said Ash.

"Ty Nado," I said. "That uniform belongs to Ty Nado!"

Ash looked confused. "I don't know who that is."

"He's better known as *Tongue*nado."

"He eat pussy good," added Slavanka.

"Not just good," I said. "He's famous for his legendary pussy eating. And he's within our grasp! Ah! We found him!"

"Which guard is it?" asked Ash.

"Uh..." I stared at the uniform. I knew that giant uniform belonged to Sarge, so it wasn't him. But the other five were roughly the same height. It could have been any of them.

"That's not really important," said Teddybear. "Just put on the uniforms and get out of there."

"But Ghostie isn't back yet," I said. "And anyway, none of these uniforms are going to fit Ash. New plan: We'll stall for time while Simon finds Ghostie. And while we stall, you're going to send a short king our way."

"Short king?" asked Teddybear.

"Yes. A short king. You know the type. Shorter than 5'5, pure muscle. Huge cock. There's got to be at least one guard here who fits that description."

"Are you sure that's a good idea? Didn't that one guard say that he'd seen Ash's nipples back on the roof deck? If he sees them again, your cover will be blown."

"No one is going to see my nipples," said Ash.

"Girl, you've had so much banana juice today," I said as I rummaged through my makeup bag for some blush. "There is a 100% chance that you're gonna pull your tits out before this party is over."

"I absolutely will not."

I looked up at her. "Ash. Your tits are literally out *right now*."

"That doesn't sound right," she said.

I pointed to them.

"Oh, right. I was just looking to see if I thought Rookie would be able to identify me by them. I guess he's right that they are kinda light." She cocked her head and stared at her pale nipples in the mirror.

"Exactly. So I'm gonna darken them up, and then you can show off your tits all you want." I brushed some makeup onto her nips until they were a nice dark shade of pink. "There. All better." I fanned them to help the makeup set and then pulled the top of her monokini back into place.

"Just don't jump in a pool or get drenched in cum and we should be fine. Now…let's go find this mythical beast they call Tonguenado."

Chapter 12

FIRST ONE TO RIDE
Sunday, Sept 22, 2013

We walked back into the main room and pushed towards the center of the circle that the bridesmaids and the bride had formed.

I was super confused by what I saw inside the circle.

Some bridesmaids were bumping and grinding against the strippers, but none of them were getting fucked. Yes, grinding up against a thick cock felt nice. But this was a bachelorette party, not a 5th grade ice cream social. The whole point was to get cheered on by all your friends while you got fucked by a huge cock. Or at least to suck some dick. That was a must. Single Girl Rule #41: Any girl who doesn't suck a cock at the bachelorette party is uninvited to the wedding. This includes the bride. No exceptions.

"Why aren't any of the girls getting fucked?" I asked.

"You better not let Autumn hear you say that," said the bride.

"Right?" I said. "I can't believe Autumn almost ruined our fun by calling the front desk."

"Her husband is pretty strict. If he found out that she was in a room with strippers, he'd lose his mind. Even if she has been hiding behind a curtain this entire time."

I looked over at the row of curtains across the windows. "Should we go tell her it's safe to come out?"

"Yeah. Autumn!" called Chloe.

The curtains didn't move.

"Autumn!" she called again.

"I'll go get her," said Ash. She ran over and pulled the curtains back. But Autumn wasn't there.

"Has anyone seen Autumn?" shouted the bride over the music.

The girls stopped grinding.

"Hey," said Poker. "Why'd you stop?" He tore his blindfold off. The other guards did the same.

"The matron-of-honor is missing," said Sloane in her fancy accent.

Poker looked around. "I don't see Bandit either."

"Oh God," said Chloe. "That pervert is probably chasing her all over the hotel right now."

"Or she's on her knees somewhere like a proper bridesmaid," I said. If banana juice had the same effect on her as it had on Ash, there was a very good likelihood that Autumn was currently blowing Bandit.

Chloe shook her head. "No freaking way."

"We'll find out soon enough," I said. "Let's check all the rooms."

We all started opening doors. It was a big suite, so there were plenty of rooms to check. The first bedroom I looked in was empty. So was the second. But then I got to a big changing room, which was actually a pretty awesome idea for a bachelorette suite. There were tons of closets along one wall, vanities in the middle, and floor length mirrors on the opposite side. And pressed up against one of those mirrors was...

Holy shit, girl!

Autumn was bent over with her hands pressed against a floor length mirror. Her monokini was pulled down to expose her breasts. And Bandit was standing behind her with one hand over her mouth while the other pulled on her two red braids as he absolutely *railed* her.

I thought she'd immediately freak out that she'd been caught, but then I realized her eyes were closed.

I put my finger to my lips and shushed the other bridesmaids as I waved them all into the changing room to see what was going down with Autumn.

Chloe's jaw dropped when she saw what was happening. "Oh my God," she whispered.

"Holy shit," said another girl. "Is he fucking her?"

"Definitely," said Chloe. She pulled out her phone and started filming it as we all crowded around to watch. "Her husband is gonna kill her."

"Bandit might kill her first," whispered Poker. "Look at how hard he's fucking her. I dunno if I've ever seen tits bounce that much."

"His cock won't kill her," said Snake. "But mine might. Think she'll let me take a turn next?"

"Probably," said Poker. "She's definitely a freak. She even put her heels on just to fuck him."

Shit, he's right. She'd pretended to be such a good girl with her bare feet and sarong. And then the first chance she got, she'd snuck off and put on her heels to get fucked by a huge cock.

"Hot damn," said Rookie. "I thought you guys were joking when you said we'd get our dicks wet at parties."

"Shhhh," I hissed. I didn't want them to disturb Autumn before she came.

"You like that?" groaned Bandit. He still had his blindfold on, so he didn't know they had an audience either.

Autumn said something but it was muffled by his hand.

"What was that?" asked Bandit. He moved his hand to her hip.

"God I love your cock," she panted. "You're so fucking big."

Bandit thrust harder and her eyes flew open.

"Oh fuck," she moaned. And then she looked in the mirror and saw the reflection of all of us watching. Her eyes got huge.

She tried to wriggle away, but Bandit had a pretty tight grip on her braids. And his other hand didn't look like it wanted to leave her hip.

"Yeah, Autumn!" yelled one of the bridesmaids. "Get that dick!"

The rest of us cheered.

The noise startled Bandit and Autumn was able to slide out of his grasp. She pulled her top back up and shifted her bottom back over her pussy.

"That wasn't what it looked like," she said. "I was just uh…cleaning the mirror." She wiped her hand on the mirror, but all it did was bring attention to the fact that there were two handprints on it.

"Oh really?" asked Chloe. "Because it looked like that stripper was fucking the hell out of you."

"Nope," said Autumn. "Definitely not."

"It's nothing to be ashamed about," said Bandit as he offered Autumn one of his orange bracelets. "Married girls are always the first ones to ride a cock at a bachelorette party."

"I'm not taking that," she said. "Because nothing happened. We were just dancing."

"You call this dancing?" asked Chloe. She pulled up the footage on her phone. "Maybe I should send this to your husband to see what he thinks is happening?"

"Don't you dare!"

Chloe laughed. "Then admit it!"

"Gah, fine! I may have let him fuck me for a second. But that was the game. Pin the tail on the bridesmaid."

All the girls stared at her.

"Five of you got fucked too, right?" she asked.

"No," said Sloane. "We all just danced with our strippers."

"Seriously?!" said Autumn. "Fuck! What about those rules? Wasn't there something about any girl who doesn't get fucked at the bachelorette party doesn't get to come to the wedding? I was just following the rules."

Autumn was such a stellar bridesmaid. "Yup. Single Girl Rule #41. Any girl who doesn't suck a cock at the bachelorette party is uninvited to the wedding. This includes the bride. No exceptions."

"Yeah! That one!"

"Those were a joke," said Chloe.

I gasped. "The Single Girl Rules are not a joke."

"Really?" she asked.

"Really."

"See?" said Autumn. "As of now, I'm the only girl who gets to go to the wedding. But it's okay, I'm sure you guys can all still get invited. You," she said, pointing to Poker. "Hand those blindfolds out again and let's go for round 2."

"It would be unprofessional of me to host the same game twice," said Poker.

Autumn glared at him.

"But I do have plenty of other games we can play."

"Will they end with Chloe getting fucked?"

"Maybe," said Poker. "Everyone, follow me!" He led us to the private pool attached to the room. Bandit hopped in the shower to clean off his cock while the other guys set up six chairs around the circular pool in the center of the room.

"What do you think we're gonna play?" asked Ash.

"I'm not sure. Fuck, fuck, goose?" God, and which one of these guys was Tonguenado?

"How do you think that's played? I don't want to misinterpret the rules like Autumn did. Do we all bend over those chairs and get fucked by Snake?"

What now? "Is that how you want to play?" *Damn, girl.*

"What? No," said Ash with a nervous laugh. "Of course not." But the way she was staring directly at Snake's cock during this entire conversation told me a very different story.

That banana juice was really hitting her and Autumn hard. And I was loving it for them.

"Gather round, ladies," called Poker. "This game is called Musical Cocks. It's just like musical chairs, but instead of a chair, you'll all be sitting on our laps. Any questions?"

Autumn raised her hand. "So to be clear…we're supposed to ride your cocks, right?"

"Nope," said Poker. "I really just meant laps."

"Matron-of-honor is huge slut," said Slavanka.

"Yeah she is!" I went to high five Autumn, but she left me hanging.

"I'm not a slut. I just don't want Chloe to be able to hold this over me for the rest of my life. There's no way I'm going to walk out of here being the only one to fuck a stripper. I would literally die."

"Sorry, girl," said Chloe. "But I'm not gonna fuck anyone. My fiancé would kill me."

"Your loss," said Poker. "Time to play!" Some music started playing and each stripper took a seat in one of the chairs around the pool.

I grabbed Ash's hand and we started walking around the circle. Some of the other girls joined us, but Chloe was not among them. Which was weird, because as my doppelgänger, I would have expected her to be way cooler. Especially at her own bachelorette party. She was being so dismissive of the Single Girl Rules too.

"Do you think I'm going to be lame in the future?" I asked Ash.

"No way."

"But Chloe is being so lame."

Ash shrugged. "Maybe her fiancé has a bigger cock than all these guys."

"I hope that's it. If not, then we were definitely sent here to save these girls with the Single Girl Rules."

The music stopped and I jumped onto the nearest lap, which happened to belong to Sarge. I'd never felt such a meaty thigh before. I expected Ash to be on the guy next to me, but she'd ran all the way around the pool and sat on Snake. *Naughty girl!* She definitely had the hots for him. The only question was…was he worthy of taking her virginity? If he was Tonguenado, then the answer was definitely yes.

I tried to think of a way to get Sarge to tell me which one was Tonguenado, but right now he thought that I worked here. Which meant I should know their names. I'd have to think of another way to find him…

"Bold move to not sit on a lap," said Poker to Chloe.

"Why?" she asked. She was leaning against the wall with her arms crossed.

"Did I forget to mention what the winner gets?"

"Let me guess. The winner gets fucked?"

Poker laughed. "If she chooses to. In musical cocks, the winner can get fucked by the last stripper remaining. Or she can have him fuck one of the girls who lost."

Chloe stared at him.

"Good news, though. We each have two legs, so you're not out of it yet."

Sloane was on one of his legs. But his other leg was unoccupied.

Chloe ran for it, but another girl beat her there.

"Shit!" she screamed as she searched for another leg. The only one left was Sarge's leg opposite me. And she made it there just in time.

"I knew you'd want to play," said Poker.

"I'm not playing," said Chloe.

"Sure you are. You sat on a lap, thus you've agreed to follow all the rules."

She looked to me for help.

"Sorry, girl," I said. "But he's right. If you'd chosen not to play then you wouldn't have been at risk of losing. But now you're in it."

"Damn it! Okay, let's do this. I hope you're ready to get fucked again, Autumn."

"No way!" yelled Autumn from across the pool on the tatted guy's lap. I hadn't gotten to interact with him much. Could he be Tonguenado? All I knew was that Tonguenado was amazing at eating pussy and didn't give a fuck if the girls he ate had boyfriends. And anyone with that many tattoos probably didn't give many fucks... It could definitely be him. I made a plan to try to linger on him and end up on his lap in the next round.

And then the perfect plan came to me.

I was going to find Tonguenado, and then when I won this thing, I was gonna send him straight for Ash's virginity. Honestly, I didn't really have a choice. Single Girl Rule #13: Always wing woman for the girl with the longest active dry spell. And a lifetime was one hell of a dry spell. #AshIsDry.

"Time for round 2?" I asked.

"Not quite," said Poker. "First we have to eliminate one of the cocks."

"And how do we do that?"

"It'll vary by round, but for round 1…the last guy to get his dick touched is out. So ladies…if you like the man your sitting on, grab that dick."

"Safe," called Snake.

I looked over and Ash had gone right for his dick. *Get it, girl!*

Slavanka wasn't shy about grabbing Poker's dick. And Sloane kept Bandit in it.

"Grab my cock," barked Sarge.

"Excuse you," said Chloe. "You can't just ask a girl to grab your cock."

I didn't reach for it either. Sarge was hot and all…but I knew he wasn't Tonguenado. So I didn't mind if he got eliminated.

And as soon as the other two guys yelled, "Safe," Sarge was out. We stood up and he removed his chair from the side of the pool.

"Everyone ready for round 2?" asked Poker.

We all nodded.

"Then why do you two still have your tits covered up?" he asked, staring at me and Chloe.

"Uh…why wouldn't we?" asked Chloe.

"Because your guy got eliminated. That's the rule. Whoever is on the lap of the guy who goes out has to take her tits out as punishment."

"You're definitely just making this stuff up," said Chloe.

"I swear I'm not."

Geez, Chloe. Stop being so lame. "Come on," I said. "Let's do it." I slid the straps of my suit down my arms and let my tits spill out. I was very disappointed in Chloe's behavior. I definitely did not want to be her when I grew up. But at the same time, I couldn't be more excited for Ash. Because Autumn was a fucking slut! Ash was going to be even more fun when we were....well, however old these girls were. Early 30s, probably.

Chloe sighed and did the same.

There we go! She was finally acting like a proper bride.

"Any other rules we should know about in advance?" asked Chloe.

"Nope," said Poker. "Well, maybe just one."

"Which is?"

"From here on out, you aren't gonna be sitting on laps. When the music stops, any girl without a cock in her mouth is out."

Ah, yasssss! Now that was my kind of game.

"Good luck!" he said. The music started playing and stopped a second later.

I'd been planning to make it to the tatted guy, but I'd hardly had any time to get there. The closet stripper was Poker, so I dropped to my knees and wrapped my lips around his beautiful cock.

"Okay, boys," he said, looking around at his friends. "First one to…" He stopped mid-sentence as I took him into my throat.

I smiled to myself.

When he started talking again, I took him even farther.

"Fuck," he groaned.

I stayed down for a second and then eased up so he could focus on whatever it was he had to say.

He took a deep breath. "First one who's girl stops sucking first is out."

There was no way I was going to stop first. His cock was exactly what I'd been craving. And the fact that he hadn't cum immediately when I jammed him down my throat made me think he might be Tonguenado. Because anyone who had perfected the art of pussy licking had also probably learned how to not cum in two seconds from a great blowjob.

"Ah!" yelled Sloane. Her posh Spanish accent even came through in that single word.

I looked to my left and saw Sloane pulling back from Rookie's cock with cum spilling out of her mouth.

"How dare you cum in a duchess' mouth?!" She slapped him and then shoved his chest, sending him toppling backwards into the pool. I pulled my lips off of Poker so I could get a better look at what was going down.

"Damn it, Rookie," said Sarge. "I taught you better than that." He waded into he pool and grabbed his arm. "Get your sorry ass out of there and hit the showers. NOW!"

"Yes, sir," muttered Rookie.

"Alright, maid-of-honor," said Poker. "Your man is out, so let's see those tits."

"*Royal* tits," she corrected as she slid her straps down.

"Speaking of royalty," said Poker, "it looks like our bride has been eliminated."

She wasn't the only one who had gotten out that round. There had been twelve legs to sit on in the first round, and only five cocks to suck in round two. So seven girls had gotten out. Including Ash.

The poor girl looked so sad standing on the sidelines while we had all the fun.

"Don't worry, Ashniqua," I said. "If I win, I'm gonna send a beautiful cock your way."

She turned bright red. But she didn't run and hide. So she definitely wanted it.

"And if I win," said Autumn, popping up from Snake's lap and staring right at Chloe. "You're gonna get fucked so hard."

"Wow," said Poker. "I'm loving this competitiveness. What about our other three contestants? Who are you playing for?"

"I fuck Ashniqua," said Slavanka.

I assumed that meant she was gonna have a stripper fuck Ash if she won, but I wasn't sure. She could have just as easily been referring to a strap-on situation. After seeing her Russian nibbles blowjob technique, I had no idea what kind of kinky shit she was into.

"I'm with Autumn," Sloane said. "If I win…Chloe is getting fucked."

"What?!" yelled Chloe. "Traitor!"

"I am no traitor," gasped Sloane. "My great grandfather fought loyally alongside King Alfonso XIII, and my grandfather helped Franco restore the monarchy."

Sloane loves Fransisco Franco? The only other girl I knew who so openly professed her love for a dictator was Slavanka. These girls really were our doppelgangers. Which really made me think that Slavanka was a secret Russian Princess. But that didn't matter nearly as much as the fact that my doppelganger was a total party pooper. I was getting seriously concerned about what this meant for my future. In addition to having Tonguenado take Ash's virginity, I desperately needed to help Chloe see the magic of the Single Girl Rules.

"She's not being a traitor," I said to Chloe. "She's just doing her job. Single Girl Rule #39: Being a maid of honor is the most scared duty in a woman's life. And also…don't forget Single Girl Rule #40: At a bachelorette party, every girl is single again."

"Yeah we are," agreed Indigo, the other girl still in the game. "When else are you gonna have a chance to get dick this good? And don't pretend like your husband is some sort of stallion. My man saw him in the locker room, and…" She held up her fingers and spread them a measly few inches apart.

Oh God no! If this was a glimpse of my future, then my worst fears were coming true. I wasn't used to feeling such dread in my chest. Was this how Ash felt all the time? I hated that for her.

"Time for round 3!" yelled Poker. The music started up yet again. The five of us walked around and around the beautiful naked men.

Are you Tonguenado? I thought as I passed each one of them. I could guess cock size from a mile away, but it was harder to tell when a guy would be great with his tongue.

I eyed Snake as I walked passed him. His nickname might be referring to his huge cock. Or the fact that he's sneaky like a snake. But it could also be because his tongue moved like a snake when he was eating pussy.

Gah!

Or maybe Bandit was Tonguenado. He *did* have a thing for married women. And I knew that Tonguenado liked stealing boys' girlfriends in college…

Or could it be Poker, the gamemaster? I could definitely see him making a game out of how quickly he could make a girl come using only his tongue.

Or finally, was it this mysterious man with the tattoos? I hadn't heard anyone say his nickname yet. It was possible they all called him Tonguenado.

The music stopped and I was closest to the tattooed guy, so I ran over to him and got on my knees. I was surprised when I felt a cold metal stud on the underside of his tip.

Oooh! What a lovely surprise!

I flicked my tongue against it and he moaned.

"You like that?" I asked.

He nodded.

"How are you with your tongue?"

He raised an eyebrow. "Win this game and maybe I'll show you."

I liked his confidence. But that didn't mean much. All guys thought they were great at eating pussy. It didn't mean they actually were.

I ran my hands over his tattooed abs and licked his cock from balls to tip.

Maybe if I got lucky the losing guy this round would be determined by some sort of face sitting...

"This round is the bride's choice," said Poker.

"So I just get to choose who I eliminate?" asked Chloe.

"That's right. Now's your chance to get rid of a guy that you don't want to fuck. You know...since three out of the four remaining girls have all said they're gonna have the last stripper left fuck you if they win."

Shit. Slavanka got out? I looked around for her, but she was nowhere to be seen. Damn it, now I was the only one trying to get Ash her first D.

"Hmm...let's see..." Chloe walked around the circle of chairs, staring at each man's cock as she went. She took a step towards Bandit like she was going to choose him, but then she ran back to Poker and pushed him backwards into the pool.

He popped up a second later, spitting water and wiping his eyes.

"Damn," he said. "What was that for?"

"Your punishment for making up the rules as we go. And my fiancé would kill me for fucking any of you, but he'll doubly kill me for fucking a super-hot black guy."

"Girl, same," I said. "#MyBoyfriendMightBeRacist." She really was my doppelganger.

"Makes sense," said Poker. "After all, the saying is true. Once you go black, you never go back." He winked at her.

"That's bad news for Autumn's husband then," said Chloe.

"Don't get too confident," said Autumn. "Bandit is still in it."

"Damn right," said Bandit. He looked over at Chloe. "Those beautiful tits are just begging to be covered in my cum. But don't worry…first I'll bend you over and make you come on my cock like the whore that you are."

Hot damn. I hoped my maid-of-honor got me strippers like this some day at my bachelorette party.

"Let's see what happens," said Poker. "Let round four begin!"

I expected the music to start, but nothing happened. *What the hell is going on?*

Chapter 13
MUSICAL COCKS
Sunday, Sept 22, 2013

We all looked around. And then Slavanka walked out from behind the frosted glass of the showers. She was holding a sign that said ROUND 4, like she was the ring girl at a boxing match. She did one lap around the pool and then disappeared back into the shower area.

Then the music started. Us four remaining girls - me, Indigo, Sloane, and Autumn – all danced around the pool.

Tattoo man had been interesting, but I'd already tasted him. So I sped up when I was in front of him and slowed down when I was near Bandit or Snake.

When the music stopped, it was Snake's lucky day.

And mine. Because his cock was just as delicious as I'd expected. Not only was it long, but it was fucking *thick*. I was a pro though, so I'd properly prepared. Instead of getting on my knees, I'd arched my back and bent over. The angle helped me open up my throat so I could take every inch of him.

"Told you I wasn't a virgin," I said when I came back up for air.

He smiled down at me. "Hmmm…I'm still not sure. Just because you're blowing me doesn't mean you've had sex."

"Your tricks won't work on me, Snake."

"Oh really? I have a feeling you'd love to see all my tricks." There was a sexy glint in his eye. "I bet you're soaking wet for me." He grabbed my monokini and yanked me closer. And then he slid the bottom of it to the side and slid his finger deep inside of me. "See?"

Fuck yes. "Of course I'm soaking wet. Last round I got to suck a pierced cock." I bit my lip and looked over at tattoo man.

"Ha," he scoffed and swirled his finger inside of me.

Oh God.

"You really think I'd believe that you like Sketch's cock better than mine? That thing is tiny."

Of course I didn't like Sketch's cock better than Snake's eleven-inch monster. But I had just tricked him into telling me tattoo man's nickname. I was determined to figure out which of these beautiful men was Tonguenado before we escaped. Speaking of which…I hadn't heard from Teddybear in a while.

I deepthroated Snake again. And then I popped up and looked him in the eye. "Status report?"

"Huh?" he said. "Are you asking if I'm about to cum? If so, then the answer is no. I may be a snake, but I always make a lady come first."

Hmmm… Spoken like a true Tonguenado.

"No word from Simon," said Teddybear into my earpiece. "But I think I've located a short king in the building. Hang in there."

Hang in there? With pleasure. Did Teddybear not realize what I was doing right now? He must not, because usually he got super jealous about these things. Or maybe he'd just finally accepted that listening to me with other guys was super hot. I bet he couldn't wait to see some pictures, that naughty boy. I kept sucking Snake as he slipped another finger inside of me.

"Which guy gets eliminated this round?" asked Chloe. "Do I get to choose again?"

I tried to focus on the conversation even though Snake's fingers were driving me crazy.

"Nope," said Poker. "This round is contestants' choice. The three remaining girls get to vote on who to eliminate."

"Easy choice," said Autumn. "We keep Bandit and Snake."

"Why them?" asked Poker. "Sketch was your man this round, so eliminating him will mean you have to take your tits out."

Autumn shrugged. "You've all seen them already. I'll do whatever it takes to make sure Bandit stays in. Otherwise I'm never going to be able to play never have I ever with Chloe again. The two cocks things is already bad enough, but at least my husband is in on that joke."

"Ooooh," said Chloe. "Good idea. She poured out a shot of banana juice and walked over to Autumn. "Never have I ever...been fucked by a big black cock at a bachelorette party."

Autumn gave her the finger and then took the shot. "And Snake is a good backup plan. Because if she wans to use the big black cock thing, I'll be able to hit her back with never have I ever rode an eleven-inch cock."

Poker nodded. "Excellent reasoning. What about you two?" He looked over at me and Sloane.

I guess Indigo had been too slow to shove a cock down her throat this round.

"I agree to keep Bandit, but my other vote is to keep Sketch," Sloan said. "A man with a piercing is quite an interesting treat."

Poker turned to me. "It's up to you then. Do we keep Sketch or Snake?"

Snake hooked his fingers inside me and then slowly pulled out. "Keep me in and I'll let you come," he whispered. His finger brushed against my clit for just a second before he dropped his hand back down to his side.

Hmmm. Dirty tease. I had a lot to ponder here. While I was thinking, Ash ran over to me. "Please keep Snake," she whispered. "I want him to be my first." She looked down in awe at his giant cock as she put back another shot of banana juice.

She didn't even turn red when she said it. Which made me wonder how much banana juice she'd had.

That was a lot of meat for such a little girl, but if Ash wanted it… "I got you," I said. "I vote that we keep Bandit and Snake."

"Alright," said Poker. He turned back to Autumn. "Sketch is out. Let's see those tits."

She pushed Sketch into the pool and then pulled her tits out.

"Those the ones?" asked Sarge over in the corner.

Rookie shook his head. "Nope. Too dark to be hers."

Slavanka came back out of the showers with a sign for round five. She did her lap around the pool and then the music started.

Only me, Sloane, and Autumn were left. And we were all trying hard to win. We'd each go super slow in front of each guy and then run as fast as we could to the next one.

The music stopped.

Autumn was right by Snake so it was only a split second before his cock was in her mouth. But me and Sloane were caught in no-man's land. She was on one side of the pool, and I was on the other. And right between us was Bandit with his delicious cock sticking straight in the air, just begging for one of us to come wrap our lips around it.

I ran as fast as I could, but Sloane was a formidable foe. We each arrived at the same time. But then she made a critical error and grabbed for his cock. I, on the other hand, went mouth first. My momentum sent his cock all the way down my throat until my lips pressed up against Sloane's hands. She bent down and started sucking his balls.

"What's going on over there?" asked Poker.

"Just getting a nice double blowjob."

"You can only have one. Who was first?"

"The blonde one."

"Mierda," cursed Sloane as she pulled back. "How dare you say she was first, you useless peasant."

"You've already blown me three times," he said, pointing to the three orange bracelets on her wrist. "And she really did get her lips on me first. But I don't mind if you jerk me off while she blows me." He grabbed Sloane's tits but she swatted him away.

"You are never welcome in Spain," she said, and then she spun on her heel and walked away.

"Well then," said Poker. "We have our two final women. But the question is…who will be the final man?"

"Do I get to choose again?" asked Chloe.

Poker shook his head. "Nope. Before I announce the method of elimination…I have to ask. Who do each of you want to see in the final?"

I pointed over at Snake. He was definitely Ash's top choice for who should take her virginity. And it was a solid choice, whether he was Tonguenado or not. Because really…she could get her pussy eaten by Tonguenado any time. But she could only lose her virginity this one time. So it should be to the biggest cock available. I usually would have been worried about him ripping her in half with that thing, but she had to be dripping wet after watching us all get to suck these beautiful cocks all afternoon.

"And you?" asked Poker.

Autumn pointed at Bandit.

"So you each want to eliminate the man you're currently with. And to do that…all you need to do is deepthroat him for longer than your opponent. Whoever stays down the longest wins."

Sorry, Bandit. There was no way I was going to lose this.

All the bridesmaids who had already been eliminated split into groups. Half were watching me, and half were watching Autumn.

"Three, two, one… deepthroat!" yelled Poker.

I took a deep breath and went all the way down.

Bandit thrust his hips forward to try to surprise me, but I was ready for it. I didn't even gag.

Just to mess with him, I grabbed his hands and put them on the back of my head, forcing him to shove me down farther.

And I still didn't gag.

"Damn, girl," said one of the bridesmaids.

I bounced up and down a little to make the show ever better.

"Oooh her eyes are starting to water!" said another girl.

"Ah! Autumn loses!" yelled a girl from the other group.

I could hear Autumn gasping for air.

It felt good to win, but to be honest, it hadn't been a fair fight. Autumn wouldn't have stood a chance in a fair fight, and this was hardly fair. Because even though Bandit was impressive, Snake was a monster.

I was impressed that she'd lasted as long as she had.

"Damn," said Bandit. "So I'm out?"

"Yup." I gave him one more lick and then pushed him back into the pool.

Poker repositioned Snake's chair to be right at the front of the pool and then put Autumn and I into position on either side.

"Ladies and gentlemen," yelled Poker, "welcome to the main event. In the blue corner, with blonde hair and a bride squad monokini, we have Charlotte, fighting to get Ashniqua fucked. And in the red corner, with red braids and the matron-of-honor monokini, we have Autumn, fighting to get the bride fucked. This fight will be one round. When the music stops, the first girl to get her mouth on Snake's cock wins."

Slavanka walked out of the showers with a round 6 sign, and Sloane was right behind her. They each walked around opposite sides of the pool and met at Snake in the middle. I thought they were just going to keep going around, but instead they tossed their signs to the side, bent over, and each licked one side of his massive cock from the balls to the tip. And then they kissed him on the cheek and strutted away.

"Blue corner ready?" asked Poker.

I nodded.

"Red corner ready?"

Autumn nodded.

"Then let's begin." The music started and we both started walking. As long as the music didn't stop when Autumn was right in front of him and I was all the way on the other side of the pool, I was pretty sure I'd win. There was no way she would run as fast as I could in heels.

"Pssst," said Ash as I passed her. "Please win!" As she said it, she spilled a little banana juice on her breasts.

Uh oh. I hoped my makeup on her nipples would hold, but I wasn't sure... I squinted to try to see if it was running off. And then I realized the music had stopped.

Shit!

Chapter 14

DOUBLE OR NOTHING
Sunday, Sept 22, 2013

I sprinted towards Snake, but Autumn had a huge head start. Luckily for me, she was terrible at running in heels. But the distance was still too much. She got there *just* before me and made sure to bury his cock in her mouth.

Damn it!

"Ladies! We have a winner!" called Poker.

Autumn popped back up. "YES! I won!"

Poker walked over and handed her a penis trophy. "I probably don't need to ask, but… Who do you want Snake to fuck?"

She smiled and pointed right at Chloe.

Chloe tried to run, but her bridesmaids grabbed her and pushed her back towards the pool.

"Nope," said Chloe. "Not happening."

Seriously? Maybe that meant I'd get to choose Ash since I was the runner up. I couldn't freaking believe I'd lost. I wanted Ash to get that D!

"But I won fair and square. I just sucked like…" She looked down at the bracelets on her wrist. "Five cocks."

"Technically only two," said Chloe, pointing to Autumn's bracelets. One was orange for Bandit but she'd #FuckedHimNotSuckedHim. One was purple for Sketch, and the other four were green for Snake. "Speaking of which…why did you keep going back for more with Snake?"

"It was random," said Autumn. "I just sucked whoever I was closest to when the music stopped."

Chloe stared at her skeptically. "Mhm. Suuuuure. Maybe you should just fuck him yourself. I promise I won't tell your husband. And I'll never mention big black cocks in never have I ever."

"Hmmm…" Autumn tapped her finger against her lips. "Tempting, but no. I worked hard for this victory."

"Too bad. That's my only offer. Take it or leave it."

Autumn turned to Poker. "Can she just refuse to get fucked? That's gotta be against the rules."

"I mean…it's certainly unsporting for her to refuse. But Snake isn't gonna rape her. If she says no, then that's that."

"But I can't be the only girl to get fucked today! That makes me look like such a slut."

He snapped his fingers. "I have an idea," he said.

"Oh?" asked Autumn.

"How about we play another game and do double or nothing. If Chloe wins, she doesn't have to get fucked. But if Autumn wins…the bride gets *two* cocks."

"Done," says Autumn. "Let's do it."

Chloe let out a sigh. "Okay, that's fair. BUT I have one condition. If I win…Autumn takes the two cocks. We all know how badly she's wanted that after groping those two men."

Autumn nodded without even skipping a beat. Which made me think that she really did want two cocks. And I couldn't blame her. Getting double teamed was fucking amazing. I immediately thought about Ghostie and Teddybear. *Hm. Weird.* I'd been double teamed a lot recently with hot randos. But whenever I thought about being double teamed, I pictured Ghostie and Teddybear. God I loved sliding back and forth on their two thick cocks. And I really loved the way Ghostie's fingers dug into my skin, bruising me. And how Teddybear's fingers tangled in my hair as he set the pace. My hot bodyguards came up a lot in my wandering thoughts recently. And I had no idea what that meant. Probably that I needed to be railed.

The girls shook hands and then turned to Poker.

"So what's the game?" asked Autumn.

"A bachelorette party classic: truth or dare. You each get to select a team. First team to fail a dare loses. Autumn, since you won musical cocks, you get to choose to be on attack or defense. The attacking team has an advantage because they get to go second and only need to complete three dares total. The defensive team has to go first and must complete *four* total dares. But if they complete all four of their dares, they win. Which do you want to be?"

"It would suck to complete all our dares and lose, so I'll pick defense."

It would be bad to lose three dares too... I was pretty sure her rationale had to do with how much banana juice she'd had.

"Excellent choice," said Poker. "For teams, we'll do a schoolyard pick. You choose first, Autumn."

"I want her," she said, pointing to Slavanka. "She seems like she's down for anything."

"Yes, yes," said Slavanka. She went to stand by Autumn.

"For me there's really only one choice after seeing that deepthroat competition," said Chloe. "I'm gonna take our bachelorette party MC, Charlotte."

Good choice. Well, kind of. It was a good choice because I was amazing at everything and down to do whatever dare they might throw at me. But also a bad choice because I kind of wanted the bride to lose and get double teamed...

Autumn picked Sloane next, and then it was Chloe's turn to pick again.

"Pick Ashniqua," I said.

Chloe looked at me like I was crazy. "The timid ginger who wanted to play trivial pursuit?"

"That was before she drank banana juice. Now that she's had some shots, she's a freak."

"If you say so…" Chloe pointed to Ash, and then Autumn rounded out her team with one of the other bridesmaids. I didn't know her name, but she'd been cheering pretty enthusiastically all night whenever a bridesmaid did something naughty.

Poker nodded. "Okay, the teams are locked in."

Autumn's team needed four people because they had four dares to complete. And we only needed three for three dares.

Poker walked over to a storage closet and wheeled out a big board of dares.

"What the hell is that?" asked Sarge.

"My dare board."

"I can see that, you fucking doughnut. I meant *why* was it in that storage closet?"

Poker shrugged. "I figured we'd need it for a bachelorette party at some point. And it looks like I was right." He turned to Chloe. "You're the attacking team, so you choose the first dare."

I scanned the list. Poker was a pro at what he did, so I knew that the names would give little hints about what the dare might be, but none of them were obvious.

Like…what was the John Hancock dare? Was a girl gonna have to recite the declaration of independence before a stripper could make her come? Or maybe the John referred to a guy who hired prostitutes and whoever did it was gonna have to go ask a stranger to pay her for a handjob. There could also be a signature involved…

And what was the Queen's Throne dare? It had to involve face-sitting, right?

"Let's see them do the Pretzel Dip," said Chloe.

Poker nodded and turned to Autumn. "Okay, defending team. Who on your team would like to try the Pretzel Dip dare?"

"I do it," said Slavanka.

Poker grabbed the envelope labeled Pretzel Dip and handed it to Slavanka.

She opened it and read, "Act out your favorite sex position with the stripper you'd most like to fuck."

Oooh. This should be good. I didn't know what position she was going to choose, but I had a feeling it was going to be way weirder than the pretzel dip, which of course was just doing a headstand, crossing your legs Indian style, and then having a guy dip his cock into you.

Slavanka walked over to Sarge, grabbed his cock, and led him to be right in front of the board.

"I need fake mustache," she said.

"Like a twirly one?" asked Poker.

"No, no. Big, manly mustache. Very furry. Like Stalin."

"Sorry," said Poker. "I have a few props stored, but no Stalin staches."

Slavanka shook her head. "Very bad." She sounded so disappointed with him.

"Can you do it without it?" asked Poker.

"No, no. That would be insult to Russia. I do the Ballerina Nutcracker instead."

Sarge gulped as Slavanka started opening and closing her jaw like she was a nutcracker.

What the hell is she about to do to this poor man?

She grabbed his right foot and pulled it up until his toes were resting on his left calf, just below the knee. And then she pushed his big beefy arms up above his head.

"Well that was unexpected," whispered Chloe as Sarge struck a very clumsy ballerina pose.

Slavanka bent over in front of him, went up on her toes, and threw one leg back over his shoulder. Then she put her arms up like she was flying.

"Grab my arms," she commanded.

Sarge did.

"Now fuck me."

He pulled her backwards. She still had her monokini on, so there was no penetration. But the bits lined up. It was actually quite an elegant position. Until Sarge lost his balance.

Slavanka swung her leg around and let him topple over.

"Bad beefcake," she said with a disappointed shake of her head. "You lucky position only half done. Otherwise your nuts go crack." She made a horrifying breaking motion with her hands.

"Wow, okay," said Poker. "For the sake of Sarge's delicate nutsuck, we should probably call that dare complete and move onto the next one. Autumn, what dare would you like Chloe's team to complete?"

"How about… Guess Who?"

Before Poker could ask who wanted to do it, I stepped forward. "I got this," I said. I was a beast at the children's game with the same name. And I was also excellent at figuring out who's dick was in my mouth. And it had to be one of those two things, right?

I grabbed the envelope and read, "Play who's in my mouth. If you get your guess wrong, the guy gets to fuck you in the ass."

Score!

"Just to be clear," asked Chloe. "Even if she guesses wrong, she still can complete the dare by letting the guy fuck her in the ass?"

"Correct," said Poker. He grabbed a pillow for me to kneel on and then put a blindfold and noise-cancelling headphones on me. I thought he might notice the earpiece, but my tits were out, so he was probably quite distracted. *Thank you, girls!*

While I waited for a dick to hit my lips, I thought about who they might throw at me. During musical cocks, I'd sucked off each of them except Sarge and Rookie, so it seemed likely that they might choose one of those two. They definitely weren't going to choose Sketch – his piercing made him too obvious. And Snake's size would be too easy to guess. So those two were out. Bandit would also be a risky pick since I'd literally had his entire cock down my throat for at least like 30 seconds during the deepthroat challenge.

A cock pressed against my lips. I gave it a kiss and then started slowly swirling my tongue around him to feel it out.

It tasted nice and fresh, but that didn't mean anything. Any of them could have hopped in the shower and cleaned their cock off before coming over to me.

I leaned forward and started exploring the shaft. As expected, I quickly narrowed it down to Sarge or Rookie. It should have been easy to tell them apart. One was a big burly 6'5 hunk, and the other was a super fit 20-year-old without an ounce of fat on his body. But when it came to their cocks, they were surprisingly similar from what I'd seen. Both were circumcised. Both were shaved.

I shifted my weight and leaned forward more. I figured a quick deepthroating would give me all the info I needed. Either my nose would press against the tight lean muscles of Rookie, or it would press into the heftier tummy of Sarge.

But the guy moved back a bit just in time to prevent me from getting all the way to the base.

I moaned around his cock in frustration. *Damn.* It had been worth a try.

Without that info, I really had no way of telling who it was. Which meant I had a 50-50 chance of guessing right. Which was unacceptable. Not because I didn't want to get fucked in the ass. In fact, that sounded lovely. But it would be a dark stain on my reputation to lose a game of who's in my mouth.

There must be some way to tell…

Someone lifted one of my earphones off a bit.

"Ready to guess?" asked Autumn.

I shook my head and she let the earphone fall back into place. And that was all I needed to figure out how to win. Because as I shook my head, I could feel the man stiffen in my mouth.

In about a minute, I'd know who it was.

I swirled my tongue around his shaft as I started bobbing up and down on his stiff cock. I made sure to pull back almost all the way, letting my soft lips brush over his sensitive head. He got harder with each movement. I kept up the pace and then surprised him by jamming him into my throat.

That was all it took. Hot cum erupted into my mouth before I pulled back and let him drench my face.

I licked my lips and smiled up at the mystery man. "Thanks, Rookie."

Someone pulled my blindfold and earphones off. And sure enough, Rookie was standing over me.

"Damn," said Autumn. "How'd you know it was him?"

"It was between him and Sarge. I was about to guess, but then I remembered how fast he'd cum earlier." I looked up at him. "Sorry you didn't get to fuck me in the ass. But my mouth was a nice consolation prize." I winked at him. "Maybe some other time."

He smiled down at me. He seemed perfectly content with cumming in my mouth. He gave me one of his blue bracelets and then headed to the showers.

Sloane did the next dare, titled Room Service. For that, she had to order a piña colada from room service and greet the waiter wearing nothing but heels.

We all hid and watched her do it. And it did not go how I thought it would.

She opened the door for him and let him wheel a cart in. I was hoping it would somehow be the short king I ordered from Teddybear…but sadly it was not.

"Your piña colada, miss," he said and presented her with the drink. It was so obvious that he was trying not to stare at her naked body.

She took a sip and spit it in his face. "This is not what I ordered."

"I'm so sorry. Did you not want a piña colada?"

"No," she said. "I wanted a piña *cum*lada. Can you help me with that?" She stared down at his crotch.

Ah, my favorite drink!

His eyes got wide. "Anything you need, miss."

"Good." She unzipped his pants and started sucking his cock.

Just when he was about to come, she pulled away and let him finish in her drink. Then she stirred it up and took a nice long sip. "Delicioso," she said and set the drink down. "Now go." She waved him away like he was nothing.

As soon as the door closed, she took a deep bow. "That, ladies, is how a duchess deals with the help."

Impressive. And props to her for knowing what a piña cumlada was.

We all went back to the big board of dares and Autumn chose Heaven.

Poker turned to our team. "Who's going to do it? Chloe or Ashniqua?"

"I'll do it," said Ash. "I go to mass every Sunday, so I'll crush whatever this is."

It seemed unlikely that it was going to relate to religion, but I wasn't going to rain on her parade. "Get it, girl," I said and pushed her towards the board.

She grabbed the envelope and her eyes got wide.

"What does it say?" I asked.

"Spend seven minutes in heaven with the biggest cock here."

The bridesmaids all cheered. The ones closest to Snake pushed him towards her.

"Shall we hit the showers?" he asked and offered Ash his arm.

She took it and he led her away.

Holy shit! Ash was about to lose her virginity. To an eleven-inch cock.

"How can we watch them?" I asked.

Chapter 15

SEVEN MINUTES IN HEAVEN
Sunday, Sept 22, 2013

"Easy," said Poker. He walked over to a statue in the corner and moved its arm. And suddenly the frosted glass of the shower turned clear.

It had only been a second, but Ash was already on her knees sucking his humungous cock.

I thought she was gonna freak out when the glass turned transparent, but she didn't even flinch.

"Why isn't she freaking out right now?" I asked.

"Magic glass," said Poker. "It's like a two-way mirror, only it looks like frosted glass instead of a mirror."

Hot damn. I needed to tell Daddy about this immediately so we could install it in all his properties. I could think of so many sexy uses for it. Like…how cool would it be to install it the opposite way in a super public place. Obviously it would be better to just fuck in public, but the illusion of being watched even when you weren't was kinda hot too.

We all crowded around the shower and watched Ash go to town on Snake's cock.

I was so proud of her. Not only was she handling his thickness like a pro, but she kept making eye contact with him too.

He let her suck him for a few minutes before hauling her to her feet. And then he tore her monokini off of her. Literally tore it in half.

She gasped as he spun her around and pressed on her back to make her bend over. Her tits pressed right against the glass. And luckily the glass wasn't wet, so her nipple makeup didn't smear off.

Here we go!

I thought he was about to fuck her. But instead he knelt behind her and started eating her pussy.

Yes!!! I was officially the best friend ever. I'd definitely found Tonguenado to take her virginity.

Or…maybe not.

Because even though he was licking her pussy, she didn't seem to be reacting.

If this was the real Tonguenado, she would have been writhing against that glass in two seconds flat.

And he'd been going at it for at least a few minutes with hardly any reaction from her.

He was unworthy of my bestie's pussy.

As soon as the clock hit seven minutes I ran over and banged on the glass. "Time's up."

"Damn," he muttered.

Poker ran over and switched the glass back to normal just before they both walked out.

"How'd it go?" I asked.

"Fine," said Ash with a shrug. "Nothing happened."

"Oh really? Then why are you ass naked?"

"Oh uh…" She looked down. "My monokini got wet so I threw it out."

"Interesting."

The next dare was Queen's Throne, to be performed by the bridesmaid whose name I didn't know. Just as I'd guessed, Queen's Throne was all about face sitting. The lucky girl got to sit on the face of her favorite stripper for sixty seconds.

But she was dumb, so she didn't choose Poker or Bandit or Sketch – the three possibilities for Tonguenado. Instead she chose Rookie.

I wasn't expecting much from the young lad as the bridesmaid pulled her thong to the side and sat on his face, but he proved me wrong.

He had her moaning within a few seconds. And then he grabbed her thighs and pulled her closer. I couldn't see what technique he was using with his tongue, but the way the bridesmaid was throwing her head back and digging her hands into his shaggy hair made me think that he was doing a damned good job.

It didn't matter though. He was too young to be Tonguenado. So the search continued.

He *almost* made her come before the sixty second timer went off.

"Well done, Rookie," said Poker and ruffled his hair. "Only two dares left. One for Chloe, and if she succeeds, then Autumn gets one final dare to win it all. What dare will Chloe be doing today, Autumn?"

She scanned the board. I still wanted to know what the John Hancock was. But instead she chose Hater.

Chloe walked up, plucked the envelope off the board, and read it: "Plant a lipstick kiss on the stripper your boyfriend would hate the most."

One of her bridesmaids went and fetched some bright red lipstick.

Chloe applied it generously while she looked back and forth between all the strippers.

"I'm ready for that kiss," said Bandit.

"What makes you think it's you?" asked Chloe.

"Come on, it's definitely me. You said earlier that your fiancé would double kill you if you fucked a black guy. And even if that wasn't true, all boyfriends hate me."

Oh really? That sounded a lot like Tonguenado to me! Could Bandit be my man?

"He might hate me more," said Poker. "She must have chosen to eliminate me for a reason earlier. And let's be honest, I'm better looking."

"He would hate if I fucked you, sure," Chloe said. "But I think you two would actually get along quite well. He loves playing games. He and his friends even play poker once a month." She ran over and planted a big kiss right on Bandit's cheek.

"You call that a kiss?" asked Bandit. "This dare is about making your fiancé jealous. Kiss me somewhere that would *really* make him jealous."

"Kiss his cock!" started chanting Autumn. The other bridesmaids joined in.

Chloe rolled her eyes. "You girls are ridiculous. But I have to admit…you're all being good sports. So…" She dropped to her knees and planted a big fat kiss right on the side of his cock. And then she popped up and ran away from him, covering her mouth in disbelief.

The girls all cheered like crazy.

It took a few minutes for Chloe to compose herself, but eventually she came back over to the group. "If any of you ever tell a soul about that, you're dead."

"Don't worry," I said. "Single Girl Rule #7: Pics or it didn't happen. And no one got a pic of that, so…"

She let out a deep breath. "Now that's a rule that I can actually get behind. We both completed three dares. That means we tied, right? It's a draw. No one has to get fucked."

"Nope," said Poker. "We don't do ties in truth or dare."

"How is this even truth or dare?" she asked. "No one ever had an option to do a truth."

"You want Autumn to be able to do a truth instead of her final dare?"

"Hell no."

"Alright then. Please pick a dare for her to do. And pick carefully…because if she completes it, then you lose. Which means that…"

"I know what it means!" said Chloe.

"So what will it be?"

She turned back to us. "What do you girls think? Tweet Tweet? That sounds like she might have to shove a bird up her ass or something. And she loves animals, but not like that."

"Whatever you do, don't choose John Hancock," said Ash. "As a fellow trivial pursuit lover, I feel like Autumn will be able to crush that one."

"I'm not so sure," I said. "John Hancock has to do with signatures. What if that dare is to get her tits signed with a sharpie or something? That would be hard to wash off before you girls head home. She'd have to forfeit or her husband would find out."

"Damn, tough choice…" Chloe stared at the board. "Fuck it. Let's go for Tweet Tweet."

Gah, I really wanted her to pick the John Hancock one.

He grabbed the envelope off the board and handed it to Autumn.

She started to open it, but he put his hand on hers.

"Before you open that," said Poker, "let's check out the other one they were considering. Just to see what it was." He took John Hancock off the board and read: "Let Sketch tattoo his signature on your ass."

I knew it! Kind of. That was actually way more intense than what I'd guessed. But same basic concept.

"Oh hell no," said Autumn. "No way I would have done that."

"Damn it!" yelled Chloe.

Autumn gave her a sassy smile. "Sucks to suck."

"Don't celebrate yet. You still have to do *that* dare." She pointed to the Tweet Tweet envelope.

Autumn opened it and read: "Post a gif of you blowing a stripper on the Banana Party twitter feed with the caption, 'What should she do next?' Tag your boyfriend. If he responds within 5 minutes, do whatever he says and post another gif of it for him."

Chloe looked so excited. "Yes!"

"What the hell kind of a dare is that?" asked Autumn.

"A damned good one. Do you concede defeat?"

"That depends. Can I hide my face in the picture?"

"You can try," said Poker. "I'll let one of the other bridesmaids take three gifs. If you don't post one of them, then you lose."

"I got you," I said. "I'm great at filming blowjobs."

"God, I hope so."

I positioned her on her knees on a cushion in front of the pool. And checked the shot. Her tits were still out, and the words MATRON OF HONOR were visible on here black monokini just below them. The whole thing was classy AF. The perfect bachelorette party gif. Only one thing was missing.

"So who are you gonna blow?" I asked.

"Hmm…" She looked around at all the strippers. Despite Rookie having cum twice, he was still rock hard thanks to my boner darts. So any of them were an option. "How about you," she said, pointing to Bandit.

Wow. I'd thought for sure she was gonna pick Snake. But maybe she'd lost interest in him after he'd been so bad at eating Ash's pussy.

"Oh damn," said Bandit. "I knew you loved big black cock."

"I just figured that the girls already got a video of me being fucked by you. So what does it matter if they take a gif of me blowing you too?" She bit her lip and looked up at him. "And you're right… My husband doesn't know I love big black cocks. So he'll be less likely to think it's me if that's what the girl is sucking."

"I love that logic," he said. "Now suck my dick, slut. And make sure you put on a good show for your husband."

He pulled her head onto his cock and she greedily sucked him.

I looked at the screen and tried to find the perfect angle for a gif.

"Put your hand further down his base," I said. "And loosen your grip." His cock immediately appeared bigger in the frame. "When you suck, make sure you go as far back as possible to really show off his length. Arch your back a little more… Perfect!"

I took a gif. The angle was hot, but it didn't really have the party atmosphere.

"We need more people in it," I said. "Bridesmaids, go stand behind the pool so we can tell there's an audience. I'll make sure I keep your faces out of it."

The girls all ran back behind the pool. A few of them pointed to really get the point across that they were watching.

I took another gif. It was *almost* perfect. But it was still missing something.

I waved Poker over. "Stand right here," I said. "I want your cock to be in it too."

I took my third and final gif. And it was fucking perfect. Autumn was sucking Bandit's cock like a pro. Her eyes weren't visible. And in the final few frames Poker's delicious cock swung into the frame.

She popped up and looked at it.

"Damn I look hot," she said.

"You really do."

"Okay, let's post it."

A minute later, Poker hit *tweet* and the post went live.

"Oh fuck. Wait!" she yelled.

"I already posted it. What's wrong?"

"My rings," she said, looking down at her hand in horror.

Poker played the video back. Sure enough, her rings were visible.

"Take it down!"

"Are you sure?" asked Poker. "If you do, you'll lose the dare."

"Fuck, fuck, fuck." She started pacing and fanning her armpits.

"I really think it'll be fine," I said. "Guys don't notice stuff like that. Honestly he's probably more likely to recognize your tits."

She let out a sigh. "I guess you're right. And he may have already seen it. No reason to lose now if I don't have to."

"You know what would take your mind off it?" asked Bandit.

"I'm not doing anything else with your cock today."

"Unless your husband responds and says I should fuck you."

"There's no way. My husband doesn't watch porn. He's not gonna respond."

"You sure about that?" asked Poker. He stared down at the phone.

"You're kidding."

"Nope. He said, and I quote… 'Have that other black dude raw dog her until she comes. #NotCheatingIfHesBiggerThanHerHusband.' "

"No fucking way." Autumn grabbed the phone and stared down at it in disbelief. "What the fuck?"

"How do you want it?" asked Poker. He looked so excited.

"Well…" said Autumn, looking around the room. "I'm doing this to win truth or dare. So how about you bend me over in front of the board?"

"With pleasure."

All the girls gathered around to watch as Autumn slid out of her monokini and bent over, bracing her arms against the board.

"Ladies," said Poker. "Put your hands together for the slut-of-honor, Autumn!"

He stroked his cock to get it nice and hard and then slowly slid into her.

"Oh fuck," she moaned.

The girls all cheered as he fucked her. And then they started a chant of, "Faster, faster!"

I grabbed the phone and got into position to take the perfect gif whenever he made her come. But then I noticed a new notification from Twitter.

I opened it, and it was another message from her husband's account: "Oh, and when she comes, have that first guy cum in her face."

I went over and showed it to Bandit. "Think you can help with this?" I asked.

"I would love to."

He started stroking himself as we walked back over to the crowd of girls. I'd never seen a girl get fucked so hard. In fact, he fucked her so hard that the brakes keeping the dare board in place gave out. The board groaned and then rolled away. Autumn fell to all fours while Poker relentlessly fucked her from behind. I could tell she was close. I motioned to Bandit and we both got into position – me filming from the side, and him jerking off near her face.

"Oh fuck," moaned Autumn. "Harder!"

I started recording the gif just as Poker grabbed her braided pigtails and slammed into her.

Her entire body shook with pleasure. If Poker hadn't had one hand on her hips keeping her up, her legs definitely would have given out.

And just at that moment, Bandit unleashed all over her face. And when I say unleashed, I mean *unleashed*. He'd had a raging boner for at least an hour. He'd gotten to fuck her. And then he'd been blown by a bunch of hot bridesmaids, culminating with me deepthroating him for a full thirty seconds. All that pent up horniness came exploding out in damn near a gallon of cum. The first shot alone completely covered her face. She kind of dodged the second one and it ended up hitting a bridesmaid standing a good three feet away.

And then the next five shots were all back on Autumn. She put her hand up to block a few, but it didn't do much good.

Sometime in the middle of that, Poker muttered, "Oh fuck," and grabbed her hips so hard. His abs tightened and I was pretty sure he was pumping her full of cum.

I'd never heard a group of girls cheer so loud.

When it was all done, she wiped her eyes with the back of her hands and looked up at Bandit.

"What. The. Fuck?"

"Sorry, girl," he said. "Husband's orders." He took the phone from me and showed her the second tweet.

"Unfuckingbelievable," she said. "And you." She turned to look at Poker who was still fucking her from behind, albeit not as vigorously as before. "Did you seriously just cum in me?"

"Sorry about that," he said and pulled out. Cum spilled out of her.

"Jesus, dude. You're lucky I'm on birth control." She turned to me. "Please tell me you got a gif of that so that I can win the dare."

"Absolutely," I said. "And the good news is that you got covered with so much cum that there's no way your husband will know it's you."

Chapter 16

THE FEELINGS DICK

Sunday, Sept 22, 2013

Bandit and Poker helped Autumn to her feet.

"Can I have a towel?" she asked as she covered herself with her hands.

"Why?" asked Bandit.

"Uh…because I'm covered in your cum."

"But it looks so good on you."

"Ladies!" yelled Poker. "It is my pleasure to present the winner of truth or dare, the matron-of-honor, Autumn!" He took her hand and raised it into the air like she'd just won a boxing match.

All the girls cheered as I snapped a photo of her.

But then she burst into tears.

"Oh my God," said Chloe, rushing over to her. "Aut, what's wrong?"

"I just…" Autumn sniffed and tried to stop her tears. "That sex was amazing. And before that I've only ever had sex with Noah. And I couldn't stop thinking about him the whole time. And feeling so guilty for loving it. But I shouldn't feel guilty. Because I've only ever had sex with him. I've been so loyal to him." She sniffed again.

"You didn't do anything wrong," said Chloe. "This is a bachelorette party. All girls are single here, right?"

"But I don't want to be single. I love him. Or at least I loved him. Until he…" She couldn't finish her sentence through the tears.

What is happening right now? There was only one way to work through whatever this was without totally killing the vibe of the party. "Girls, circle up!" I yelled. "It's time to pass around the feelings dick."

"Feelings dick?" asked Ash. "I thought it was a feelings *stick?*"

"Right. It's like that, but with a dick instead of a stick."

"I confused," said Slavanka.

"Okay, here's how it works. We all sit in a circle, and whichever girl is holding a dick has to share their deepest, darkest feelings." I snapped at Rookie and pointed to Autumn.

He walked over and stroked himself to make sure he was nice and hard for her while the other strippers brought us all chairs.

I sat back in my chair and stared at Autumn. "Now grab that dick and tell us everything."

Autumn sniffed a few times and then reached up and grabbed Rookie's cock. "Men suck."

"Yeah," agreed Chloe. "Boys are idiots. So what did your idiot boy do?"

"A few months ago…" She paused and stroked Rookie while she thought about it. "I found texts between Noah and his secretary. Like…naked ones."

"His secretary?!" gasped Chloe. "So that's who he was with…"

"Huh?"

"Oh shit. Uh…"

"Spill it."

"Last week I left my wedding planning binder at your house. So I went over to grab it during lunch and heard some uh…noises…upstairs."

"That fucker brought her back to the house?" asked Autumn. Her tears were gone. Now she just looked pissed. Her fist tightened around Rookie's cock and his eyes got big.

"I'm sorry I didn't tell you sooner," said Chloe. "I was planning to tell you after the wedding. But then when these strippers showed up…I figured it was the perfect time to help you get that huge cock of your teenage dreams. That's why I was being kind of a bitch during the games."

"Oh my God, that makes so much sense now." And then Autumn got a funny look on her face. "Wait, back up. What do you mean huge cock of my teenage dreams?"

"Uh…" Chloe looked away like she was guilty of something awful. "So you know that journal you wrote in every night in high school?"

"Which one?" Autumn gasped. "Oh God. Please tell me you didn't read the blue one."

Chloe cringed. "I'm afraid so."

"Oh fuck." Autumn looked like she wanted to disappear.

"You *really* wanted to get railed by a twelve-inch cock at prom, huh?"

"I don't think I can ever look at you again."

"Girl, we all just watched you get railed by a stripper. And you're embarrassed about some journal?"

"Well now I'm embarrassed about all of it!"

"You shouldn't be. We all have fantasies. Fuck Noah and his stupid cheating ass. After the wedding, let's find you a beautiful foot-long dick so you can live out all your wildest fantasies. And I can live vicariously through you."

"Live vicariously through me?" asked Autumn. "I'm the one who needs to live vicariously through you. I know Harrison made you promise not to tell anyone about what you two do in the bedroom, but I've seen the way he stares at you. Your honeymoon is going to be WILD."

"Ow ow!" yelled the overly enthusiastic bridesmaid.

Chloe didn't look excited though. "I wish."

"What do you mean you wish? Wait, is Harrison not a freak? I've been completely convinced that the locked room in his house is a playroom and he's a total dom. Like with leather and whips and stuff."

Yes! Get it, girl! I loved that for future me.

"He's like the opposite of a dom."

"He's your sub?" asked Autumn. "Wow. Plot twist. Although now that you mention it, I can kinda picture him liking to be spanked…"

Chloe laughed. "No. He's not my sub. We don't do any BDSM. Or anything kinky at all, really."

No! Now I hated that for future me.

"But he's so controlling. Like how he makes you dress so conservatively. Wait, are you telling me that you don't wear leather harnesses and lingerie under all that?"

"Hell no," said Chloe. "He just doesn't want me to get hit on by random dudes. I still can't believe he bought me this." She gestured down to her very low-cut bride-to-be monokini.

I pressed my lips together. Yeah, her husband definitely wouldn't approve of the sexy monokini I'd gotten her. Oopsies. But also… #SorryNotSorry.

"It's okay," said Bandit, patting her shoulder. He'd just gotten back from the shower and had a towel wrapped around his waist. But it didn't stay there long. "Grab the feelings dick and let it all out," he said, tearing his towel away. His still-raging erection sprung up and hit Chloe in the shoulder. If I did say so myself, my boner darts were freaking amazing.

Chloe sighed and started stroking him. "Don't get me wrong," she said. "Harrison is amazing and I'm so excited to marry him. But I do kind of hate how he makes me dress. And the sex is so vanilla. I mean…it's been years since I've gotten anything except missionary."

"So?" asked Sloane. "That's what you hire the help for. My mother used to fuck our pool boy all the time."

I loved that for future Slavanka's mom!

"I can't do that," said Chloe. "As much as I love wild sex, once I walk down that aisle, I'm going to be loyal to my man." She sounded so sad about it.

"I'm so sorry," I said. I was devastated for her.

"You look like you have something on your heart," said Bandit. "Do you need the feelings dick?"

"Yes please." I motioned him over. But as he was on his way over…

"Excuse me," said Ash, raising her hand. "I need that for a moment."

Bandit stopped in front of her. I was so curious about what she was going to say. I assumed it was going to be something sappy about how I was the best friend in the whole world or whatever.

But instead she just started sucking him.

And sucking. And sucking some more.

Bandit looked at me and shrugged. And then all the girls looked at each other and shrugged too.

For a good three minutes we all just sat there and watched Ash gag on Bandit's thick cock.

But then she stopped short and looked around. She slowly slid her lips off his cock and leaned back in her chair.

"Why is everyone looking at me?" she asked.

"We were waiting for you to share your feelings."

She just stared at me.

"Because you grabbed the feelings dick."

"No I didn't."

"Girl, you definitely did. We all just watched you suck him off."

"That doesn't sound like something I would do. Is it hot in here? Why is it so hot in here?" She started fanning herself.

Girl. I stared at her. She only ever started sweating that much when she was caught in a lie or was facing a centipede.

"I was feeling horny, okay? That was my feeling! And I deeply regret my actions. Now please stop looking at me!" She shooed Bandit away.

"That is valid feeling," said Slavanka. "Thank you for sharing."

"Thank you for sharing," said all the other bridesmaids.

What the hell? When did this turn into some sort of weird AA meeting? I needed to reel this back in. "Let me show you all how the feelings dick is done. Bandit, lie down."

He lay down in front of my chair as I stripped out of my bride squad monokini. And then I sat right on his face and started stroking his cock.

"I'm feeling scared," I said. *And a little horny.* Because Bandit just slid his tongue deep inside of me and it felt fucking fantastic. But I had to stay focused. "I think that the universe brought us all together to show me and Ashniqua and Svetlana what our lives might be like in a few years. You're like our older, but still very sexy, doppelgangers. And... Oh fuck," I moaned as Bandit licked my clit and then swirled his tongue around me. I'd never felt a tongue move so fast.

"So you're scared of ending up like me?" asked Chloe.

"No, I didn't mean..." Whatever magic Bandit was working with his tongue was making me feel a little wobbly. I fell forwards a little and had to put one hand on his thigh to steady myself. "You're amazing. But you sounded so sad when you said that you were only going to get one cock for the rest of your life. I hate that for you. And since I'm your doppelganger, I hate it for me too. Especially because my boyfriend has kind of a tiny penis."

"Well, then he's not the one for you. My fiancé has a magnificent penis. He just doesn't know how to use it."

"Oh thank God," I said. "I hope that means…" I trailed off as pleasure washed over me. *Holy shit, Bandit!* He was a freaking legend with his tongue.

And then it hit me.

I'd found Tonguenado!!!

"Oh God," I moaned. I couldn't take it anymore. I leaned forward and shoved his cock into my mouth. Bending over gave Bandit a whole new angle, and he took full advantage of it. His tongue sped up even more and I shattered again.

He got me again ten seconds later. And for the first time in my life, I literally couldn't take the pleasure. I somehow got control of my legs and rolled off of him.

"So your boyfriend has a tiny penis, huh?" asked Bandit.

I nodded.

"How about I fuck you and send a pic of it to your boyfriend so he can see what a real cock looks like?"

"I'd love that. But you can't fuck me in the feelings circle. This is a sacred space for women to bond and share their deepest feelings, you pervert."

Bandit shrugged. "Then I'll fuck you somewhere else." He picked me up in his muscular arms and slung me over his shoulder.

"Ah!" I squealed as he carried me towards the door.

"Okay, enough talking about our feelings," said Autumn. "It's time for our bride to earn an invitation to her wedding."

"Huh?" asked Chloe.

I craned my neck to try to see what was about to happen.

Autumn grabbed one of the Single Girl Rules membership cards. "Single Girl Rule #41: Any girl who doesn't suck a cock at the bachelorette party is uninvited to the wedding. This includes the bride. No exceptions."

Chloe laughed. "Right. About that… I'm not gonna get double-teamed."

Autumn stared at her in disbelief. "But you promised."

"Oh well."

What the fuck? Chloe was officially NOT my doppelganger. Refusing to get fucked at your bachelorette party was bad enough, but agreeing to double or nothing and then going back on it…that was unthinkable. She was dead to me.

"I'm not going to get double-teamed," repeated Chloe. "Because that implies I'd only let two of these guys fuck me. I'm gonna let them all take a turn. Now, boys, who's first?"

Hell yeah! I take it all back. I was proud to have Chloe as my doppelganger.

Bandit paused and looked back as the other strippers all surrounded Chloe.

"I understand if you wanna go join," I said. "She is the bride."

"Fuck that," said Bandit. "The other guys can keep her busy until I'm done with you." He took me into a bedroom and tossed me onto the bed.

"You're Tonguenado, right?" I asked.

"I've been called that. I assume you've heard good things?"

"Shit," muttered Teddybear. "You gotta get out of there."

I laughed. Poor Teddybear didn't want me to have the time of my life with Tonguenado. But I'd promised him sexy pictures from this party. And I planned to deliver on that promise.

"What's so funny?" Bandit asked.

"I was just thinking about how jealous my friend sounded when he told me how you used to steal everyone's girlfriends." God, it made so much sense that Bandit was Tonguenado. I couldn't believe I didn't make that connection immediately when I found out he loved married women. All these beautiful cocks must have thrown me off my game. "Apparently you were a legend on campus for what you could do with your tongue."

"And what do you think? Did I live up to the hype?"

I stared at his perfect mouth and bit my lip. "You were okay."

"Just okay, huh?"

"Mhm."

"Let's play a little game."

"I thought Poker was the game guy?"

"He is. But he got the idea for sex games from me. Here's how it works. I'm gonna fuck you better than you've ever been fucked before. And I'm gonna take pictures the whole time. If I give you less than ten orgasms before I cum, you can delete them. But if I get you ten times or more…I'm going to send them all to your boyfriend."

"You think you can give me ten orgasms before you cum?"

He didn't answer. He just buried his head between my legs.

Oh God. My back arched off the mattress as his tongue swirled around me. Within ten seconds my legs were shaking.

"Chastity, do you hear me?" Teddybear asked. "You need to hide *right now.*"

I loved when he was jealous. But there was no way I was hiding from Tonguenado. Teddybear just needed to wait his turn. Besides, my legs were too wobbly to move right now.

Tonguenado looked up at me and smiled. "Does that answer your question?"

I nodded and raised my hips, begging for more.

"Greedy girl," he said, pushing my hips back down onto the soft mattress. "I guess that means we have a deal?"

"Yes," I said, but it came out all airy. God I needed him. And he gave me exactly what I wanted.

His strong hands massaged my thighs as his tongue explored my pussy. I raised my hips while I pushed his head down. And he didn't mind at all. He just feasted deeper.

I closed my eyes as orgasm #2 washed over me. And when I opened my eyes again I was somehow pressed up against the wall with my legs over his shoulders. Another orgasm hit me and it felt like I was fucking flying. Partially from the orgasm, and partially because he'd literally just thrown me face-first onto the bed. My face hit the fluffy pillow and a second later he pulled my hips into the air. I expected to get fucked, but instead he just kept eating my pussy, lapping up all my juices.

Five orgasms. Six. Seven. Maybe eight. I didn't know. I'd lost count somewhere between doing the splits on his face and being ass up backwards in the closet while he gave me a double- speed tonguenado.

At some point during all that I was pretty sure Teddybear had said something about more guards coming, but it hadn't really registered.

"And that's orgasm number nine," Bandit said as my entire body shook. I blinked a few times and tried to figure out where I was. We'd ended up in the changing room with the full-length mirrors, and I was bent over in front of one of them.

"My turn," I said. I got to my knees and started sucking while he snapped pictures in the mirror.

"Damn," he said as I grabbed my tits in both hands and deepthroated him. "Your boyfriend is gonna love that pic."

I smiled up at him. "Maybe. But only if you give me another orgasm."

"Oh, don't you worry. If you think my tongue was good, wait until you feel my cock."

Yes please.

It was tempting to make him cum just to teach him a lesson for being too cocky about getting me a tenth time. But then I wouldn't get to feel his cock inside of me. So that plan was out.

I stood up and took the phone from him. Then I arched my back and smiled at him. "You better give me a tenth orgasm before you cum. I'd hate for my boyfriend to not get to see the pics I'm about to take."

"Don't you worry," he said as he grabbed my hips. I snapped a pic of his thick cock sliding into me. Inch by inch, stretching me wide. I quickly forgot all about the camera. He'd awoken every nerve in my body with his tongue, and I could feel *everything*. The thick veins running along the length of his cock were driving me crazy. And when he reached around and rubbed my clit, I lost it.

"Well that was easy," said Bandit as my body clenched. The phone slid out of my hand and bounced on the floor.

"I guess we're done then?" I said, pushing him off me.

"Hell no," he said. "We're just getting started. Now pick that phone up and take more pictures. Your boyfriend needs to know how much of a slut you are."

"If you insist." I bent over to pick up the phone, and he took full advantage of it. I would have fallen over from the thrust if he didn't have such a tight grip on my hips.

Within a minute he made me come again, and then I sat him on a stool and mounted him. My tits bouncing in his face made for a lovely picture. But it made for an even better picture when he flipped me around and spread my legs wide.

He may have been known for his tongue, but his cock and fingers may have been an even better combination. In every single position he knew just the right angle to make me fall to pieces. And getting to watch the whole thing in the mirror ratcheted up the heat. I'd never seen such a fine specimen. And my partner looked decent too.

"Seriously, Chastity," said Teddybear into my earpiece. "Quit fucking around! You have to get out of there!"

Chapter 17

DICK, DICK, DICK!
Sunday, Sept 22, 2013

Gah! All of Teddybear's warnings finally caught up to me. *Run. Hide. Get out of there.* He was jealous, of course, but he was also actually warning me that guards were coming this way. I never wanted this to end. But I also wanted to see the look on the banana king's dumb face when I escaped from this hotel.

"Time for one final picture," I said. I pulled Bandit back in front of the mirrors and got on my knees.

He aimed his phone at the mirror with one hand while he stroked himself with the other.

"All over my face," I said, opening my mouth wide for his cum.

And he was happy to oblige. I'd thought that the massive amount of cum that he'd unleashed on Autumn had been a function of the boner darts and hours of pent-up teasing. But nope...that was just his normal deal.

Just like with Autumn, my face was covered with only the first shot. And then it kept coming and coming and coming. I wanted so badly to swallow down my treat, but I also wanted a perfect photo for Teddybear. No, Teddybear wasn't my boyfriend. But he deserved a special treat more that Chad. And Teddybear always fucked me so hard when he was jealous.

When I was sure Bandit was finished, I opened my eyes, gave a thumbs up to the camera, and let the cum spill out of my mouth. The contrast of the pearly white cum dripping onto my flawlessly sun-kissed tits was absolutely perfect.

"Wow," he said. "That may be the best picture I've ever taken."

"Damn right. I hope my boyfriend agrees." I took Bandit's phone, typed in Teddybear's number, and hit send.

I heard the ding of Teddybear's phone through my earpiece and then he audibly gulped.

You're welcome. I bet he'd just gotten the biggest boner.

"You should send them to yourself, too," said Bandit.

"So you can have my phone number? Nice try." I stood up, blew him a kiss, and walked out. I checked to make sure I was alone and then said into my earpiece: "What'd you think of those pictures?"

"We can talk about that later. For now, we have to get you out of there. More guards are on the way."

"Good. I'm still waiting for that short king."

"I already told you, the short king arrived twenty minutes ago. And more guards ten minutes after that. Now another squad is coming. And these guys have pictures of you."

"You can't delete it from their phones?"

"Nope."

"Shit."

"Yup. Now *please* get out of there."

"On it. Tell the girls to meet me by the door."

"I lost contact with them a few minutes ago."

"What? How?"

"From what I could gather, a particularly violent molly-whopping jarred Slavanka's loose. And I'm pretty sure Ash decided I was a demon in her head and smashed the earbud with a vase."

"Damn. She must be running low on banana juice. I'll go find her. Give me a minute." The main living area of the suite was empty, so I started checking bedrooms. Those were also empty, but the last one had a spiral staircase up to a second story. And based on the cheers coming from upstairs, I was pretty sure I'd found the girls.

"I think I found them. Hold on," I said into my earpiece as I went up the stairs.

I knew someone was gonna be getting fucked, but I hadn't quite expected *this*.

I nearly slipped on Chloe's white monokini at the top of the stairs. Or at least, half of it. The other tattered half was hanging over the banister.

The cheers grew louder. At first I thought they were cheering for me coming back from getting railed by Bandit. But no one had even noticed my arrival. All eyes were glued to Chloe taking a cumshot in the face from Sketch while Sarge took her from behind.

"Damn it," said Sarge. "You seriously couldn't have lasted another couple minutes? You're as bad as Rookie."

"I tried my best," said Sketch.

"Alright, boys," said Indigo. "Time to switch." Two other bridesmaids pulled Sarge and Sketch away. "Who's next?" she asked to...

Who the hell are they?

Seven guards were standing there, all eagerly waiting to take a turn on the bride. I only recognized Snake. The other six must have been one of the new squads that arrived. And they were just as hot as the original six. None of them were the short king that I needed, though.

Two of the new guys stepped up. One of them stared fucking her from behind while the other took her mouth.

Get it, girl! I couldn't believe that I'd doubted my doppelganger's awesomeness. She'd definitely earned her invitation to the wedding.

I wanted to stay and cheer her on, but I had to find Ash and Slavanka. I turned and looked for them amongst the bridesmaids. But they weren't there. Autumn and Sloane were missing too.

Where'd they go? It didn't make sense for them to not be here. Missing the bride getting fucked at a bachelorette party was like going to a fashion show and leaving before the robe de mariée walked down the runway.

There were a few doors out of the master bedroom, so I started looking in them.

The first was an empty bathroom.

The second was a massive walk-in closet.

And the third was a balcony overlooking the pool area. But that was empty too. Or at least, I thought it was. But then Rookie sprinted out of the shower holding an icepack against his junk. He hid behind a lounge chair just as Sloane and Slavanka burst into the room. They were both completely naked and had cum on their faces. Lots of cum. Which probably explained the icepack on his nuts. Poor Rookie hadn't been ready for this.

"No more," he yelled as Slavanka lifted up the lounge chair and tossed it into the pool.

"Svetlana," I called down. "You know there's fresh guards up here to play with, right?"

"Yes, yes," she called back. "But I like Rookie boy."

"Me too," said Sloane. "He reminds me of my mother's third pool boy. Many good memories… Although I'm not sure I'll ever get a pool boy of my own. My parents are threatening to disown me if I start my fashion label. Apparently doing any form of work is beneath a duchess."

Poor girl. Daddy was always so good about letting me follow my passions, no matter what they were. And after today, I was thinking I had a pretty strong future in bio-chem. Because even though Rookie was icing his balls, he was still rock hard.

Or at least, he had been a second ago. I couldn't see him anymore because he'd just rolled over and slid into the pool. A second later a little blue tube broke the surface and water squirted out of it. It appeared he'd torn one of his bracelets in half and converted it into a makeshift snorkel.

Slavanka turned around and looked at the spot on the floor where Rookie had been. She cocked her head to the side. And then she looked around frantically. "Where Rookie boy go?" she asked.

Sloane looked around too and then smiled. "El juego está en marcha."

The game is afoot? It was odd hearing Sherlock Holmes' classic phrase in Spanish rather than with a fancy British accent. But I had to admit, it still sounded pretty cool.

"Yes, yes," agreed Slavanka. "Game is feet."

Slavanka speaks Spanish? I didn't really know what to do with that information, but I didn't have time to dwell on it. Because Sloane was following a nonexistent trail of "clues" into some random side door, and Slavanka was about to follow.

"I'll help look for him," I said. "Give me a minute to get down there."

"No, no," said Slavanka. "You no need minute. Watch." She walked over to a statue and pulled on the arm. Part of the wall shifted to form a staircase leading down from my balcony.

Damn this place is cool. Daddy really needed to step up his game.

I was halfway down the stairs when the main door to the pool room swung open.

"Dick, dick, dick!" chanted Ash as she burst into the room. She had a bottle of banana juice in one hand, and a cock in the other. The cock belonged to a new guard. *My short king!* Ash had found just the man we needed. Although I was a little surprised to see that he was naked, blindfolded, and handcuffed to two other guards.

Autumn appeared a second later, also carrying a bottle of banana juice, and also leading a group of three hand-cuffed guards.

"Dick, dick, dick," they chanted together, getting louder with every word.

Poker was the last one through the door.

"Okay, ladies," he said. "Here's how dick, dick, dick, is played."

Is this gonna be like duck, duck, goose?

"When I say go, you start blowing your three guys. Whichever girl makes her guys cum first is the winner. Wan-na know what you're playing for?"

"Yeah!" yelled Ash.

"Winner gets bragging rights."

"Boooo!" said Ash.

"Boring!" agreed Autumn.

"Winner also gets fucked by any guy who didn't cum yet. And me." He flashed them a smile.

Okay, so nothing like duck, duck, goose. But it still sounded like a great game.

"Ready, set…"

"Hush," said Ash, putting her finger to Poker's lips. "We got this."

"Dick, dick, dick…" chanted both girls. "Go!"

I thought they were gonna both drop to their knees and get to work, but instead they each tilted their heads back and chugged what was left of their banana juice. Then they smashed the bottles on the ground, yelled, "Dick!" one more time, and *then* they started sucking.

Autumn went for the classic approach of sucking the one in the middle and jerking the other two off. Ash, on the other hand, went for a more ad-hoc strategy of sucking one for a few seconds and then switching to another.

"Fifty ruble say Ashniqua win," said Slavanka. "Prop bet of twenty ruble say short king cum third."

Slavanka is also a degenerate gambler? That kind of fit with her whole deal, I suppose. Or maybe not. Because unless the exchange rate had changed drastically in the last couple hours, fifty rubles were worth about a dollar and seventy cents.

"I'll take that bet," said Sloane. "Autumn is definitely going to win. It's much smarter to focus on one guy at a time."

They turned, nodded, and each honked the other's right breast.

Ah, a classic bachelorette's wager. It was like a gentleman's wager, but cooler.

Autumn sped up her pace for a second and then pulled back. She turned to Poker and opened her mouth. Cum spilled out onto her thigh.

"One down for Autumn!" yelled Poker.

Autumn pushed the guy backwards and brought the other two closer together. Now she was able to use her hand and mouth on one while stroking the other.

"What's going on here?" asked Bandit. He'd just come out of the shower and had a towel wrapped around his waist.

"Dick, dick, dick," I replied.

"Ah, a classic."

"Indeed. You heading up to the fuck bride?"

"I was planning on it, but now I can't."

"Oh?" I asked.

"It's part of the rules of dick, dick, dick. Any dick who enters the room during the match gets added to the winner's prize."

Ah! I love that for Ash! I'd been so focused on finding her that I'd forgotten about wanting to help her lose her virginity to Tonguenado. He'd definitely proved himself worthy of her pussy.

"Did you hear that, girls?" I called. "One more dick for the winner!"

Ash gave a thumbs up but didn't lose focus. She was still bouncing around between cocks, but she'd increased the timing so that each guy got about thirty second of her mouth before she switched off him.

I was worried for her though. Because one of the guys had just unexpectedly exploded in Autumn's hand, blasting cum all over her cheek and up into her hair.

"That's two for Autumn!" yelled Poker.

"Come on Ashniqua!" I cheered. "You got this! Play with the balls! And use your throat!"

She started playing with their balls and then stroked them hard while deepthroating the one in the middle.

The short king came first, and as expected from a short king, his cumshot was powerful. Something about his heart being closer to his dick really helped the pressure build.

"Yes!" yelled Slavanka as the short king plastered Ash's cheek in cum. "I win prop bet!"

A second later Ash pulled back and took a massive cumshot right in the eyes. And then she turned to the last guy just as he exploded all over her tits.

"Ah!" yelled Ash, jumping into the air. "Chastity! Slavanka! Did you guys see that?! I won! And now I'm gonna lose my virginity to three strippers!" She wiped some cum off her tits and licked it off her finger.

It felt like time stopped. She'd used our real names. And she'd said she was a virgin. And she'd just wiped the makeup off her nipples. Had anyone else noticed any of that? Or was it just me?

"Which one of us gets your virgin pussy?" asked Bandit, dropping his towel to the floor.

I breathed a sigh of relief. He hadn't noticed Ash's slip ups. Plus my boner darts *still* had him fully erect. Or maybe he was just excited at the prospect of getting to fuck a virgin. Either way, he was perfectly distracted.

Bandit stroked himself as he stepped towards her. But then he stopped short.

Uh oh.

"Wait a second," he said. "Weren't we looking for a red headed virgin?"

"Yeah," said Poker. "And did she just call those two Chastity and Slavanka?"

"Sure did," said Rookie. He'd emerged from the pool to watch the blowjobs. "And look at how light her nipples are. That's definitely her."

Shit! Our cover was blown! And now we were going to be caught and auctioned. Which wasn't the worst thing…

"Run!" yelled Teddybear into my earpiece. But it was too late.

Interlude

NO WAY
Saturday - Oct 10, 2026

Ash leaned forward and stared at me like I was insane. "That's quite the story. But that didn't happen."

"What detail do you dispute? Some of the dialogue may not have been verbatim, sure. But I'll never forget that epic bachelorette party. And what came next was pretty epic too."

"I dispute all of the details. Because none of that ever happened. I think I'd remember if I'd been kidnapped. Anyway, continue with your wild tales if you must, but I'm going to have more pizza." She reached for a slice, but the table between us was empty. Ash blinked and looked around. "Where'd the pizza go? And when did we get on an airplane?"

"Girl, we've been in the air for like twenty minutes. Now, what were you saying about your ironclad memory?"

Ash gave a nervous laugh. "Right. I remember taking that…fancy car to the uh…Philly airport?"

I shook my head. "We took a helicopter to a private airstrip."

"Sure did," agreed Ash with an enthusiastic nod. "I was just checking to make sure *your* memory was okay. Good news, you passed."

"Hmmm... Nope. We actually took a limo." I pulled out my phone and showed her a picture we'd taken with the hot limo driver just before boarding shmoopie poo's private jet. "Seriously, how do you not remember? Never mind," I said, snapping my fingers. "I know what happened."

"You do?"

"Yup. You must have hit your head on the steering wheel while you were giving the chauffeur road head on the way here. Very thoughtful way to tip him, if I do say so myself."

"WHAT?!"

I laughed. "Just kidding. You didn't blow him. Although I'm not sure why not. He was definitely packing something special."

"I'm a married woman! I can't just go around blowing random people."

"Right." I winked at her.

"No. Don't wink at me about that. I'm serious! And I'm also very concerned about my memory."

I waved off her concern. "It's just the banana juice messing with your head. I always thought you were joking about not remembering stuff. But now I'm thinking that your brain legit locks away all the memories you make while you're drinking banana juice. Which explains why you don't remember any of the stories I'm telling. And why you don't remember getting on this plane."

"Oh God," said Ash. "What other terrible things have I done?"

"Terrible? None that I can remember. You're actually quite sweet when you're drunk on banana juice. Unless someone gets in the way of your insatiable hunger for dick." I paused and thought back to one of my fondest memories of Ash. "You punched a bear once."

"I did what?! What situation could we have possibly gotten into where I needed to punch a bear in order to get some dick?"

"I can think of a lot of situations where that would be necessary. I mean, everyone knows that zookeepers have larger-than-average penises. That big dick energy is crucial to establishing dominance over the animals. So it's easy to imagine how punching a bear would be necessary to get that zoo keeper D. A camping trip would also…"

"I wasn't asking for hypotheticals. I wanted to know how I specifically ended up punching a bear."

"Girl, my wedding starts any minute now. We don't have time for wild stories."

"Are you kidding me right now?" asked Ash. "This whole time you've been telling the world's longest story about how I supposedly lost my virginity."

"Correction: I've been telling you a *normal length* story about how you *actually* lost your virginity. Now, shall I continue?"

"We're probably almost back to New York, so you should just skip to the end and tell me who took my V-card. I hope it wasn't that short king from dick, dick, dick."

"Why?" I asked. "What's wrong with short kings? Didn't you hear what I said earlier about the blood flow thing?"

"So it *was* him?"

"Nope." God, I couldn't wait to tell her who took her virginity. She was going to freak the fuck out.

Ash scrunched her face to the side like she did when she was thinking really hard. "Shit, I know who it was. It was freaking Tonguenado, wasn't it?"

"Maybe. That would make sense, given that you'd just won his cock as your prize for winning dick, dick, dick. But you're forgetting that the banana king had given the guards strict orders *not* to bang you. He needed your virginity intact for the auction. Speaking of the banana king...I think I'm gonna let him tell this next part of the story in his own words."

Ash gasped and looked around frantically. "Stay away, pervert!" she screamed. "I'm a married woman!"

I laughed. "Relax. He's not here. Which is a real shame. I'd love one more taste of his banana before I walk down the aisle. And I bet you'd love another ride on that thing too."

"Another?!"

I winked at her and pulled out my phone.

"Please tell me you're not calling him."

"I'm not. I'm opening up the mission report that he sent to Luigi Locatelli after the auction." I propped my phone up so that we could both watch the recording. And then I hit play.

The video started with the banana king leaning back in his leather office chair. The sun was just starting to rise over the Miami coast in the floor-to-ceiling window behind him.

"Operation Little Red Riding Virgin, status report 3," he said into the camera. "The time is..." He pushed his sleeve up to check his Rolex and I couldn't help but admire his beautiful forearms. His arm veins were unparalleled. Actually, that wasn't true. The veins in his dick were even better. But his arm veins were pretty damn sexy. "The time is 07:14 on Monday, September 23, 2013. Current location: Master office, Locatelli Resort and Spa." He paused and took a deep breath. "The mission did not go according to plan."

Chapter 18

OPERATION LITTLE RED RIDING VIRGIN
The events of Sunday, Sept 22, 2013, as told by the banana king

It had been nearly two hours since the girls had rappelled down the side of my resort. And my idiot guards *still* hadn't found them. Which was shocking, because I'd promised the boys they could do whatever they wanted with Chastity and the brunette. Ash, on the other hand, was off limits.

There was no way I was going to let my guards spoil my virginity auction. Especially after earlier. I'd exercised a level of self-control that I'd previously thought impossible.

At first it had been easy to keep my hands off of Ash. Yes, she was beautiful. But she'd been so scared of me that I hadn't even thought about doing anything sexual with her. I'd actually felt kind of bad about auctioning off her virginity.

But when I walked outside onto the terrace this morning…everything was different.

She was just lounging on the terrace in a tiny little bikini sipping on some banana juice. I'd done a lot of kidnappings, and not once had a girl ever been *this* chill about it.

Or at least…she was chill until the sun came out from behind a cloud. Then she had a mini freakout about not having enough sunscreen and ran inside screaming. But by the time I followed her inside, she was back to normal.

This was the first real test of my mental fortitude, because she tossed me a bottle of sunscreen and asked if I could rub it all over her.

She pretended to be shocked when I untied her bikini top. But then she loosened up a bit. At one point she reached for the lotion bottle and accidentally grabbed my cock. The way her face turned red with shock... So fucking sexy.

I wondered how shocked she'd look if I whipped it out. I wanted to feel her lips around my cock. I wanted so badly to taste her sweet pussy. And I wanted to sink my fingers into her long red hair. But most of all, I wanted to see the look on her face as I claimed her virgin pussy with my humungous cock.

But for the sake of the mission, I didn't fuck her. Instead I excused myself and went out onto the terrace. Luckily one of the maids was out there tidying up, and she was more than happy to let me relieve my stress all over her face.

I tried to keep my distance from Ash the rest of the morning, but she kept wanting to hang out. She was surprisingly good at ping pong. But in my defense, I was quite distracted because her tits kept falling out of her bikini top.

Anyway, despite all that, I'd managed to keep myself from fucking her.

But ever since she escaped from the terrace, fucking her was all I could think about. I'd been hard for two fucking hours straight.

I pulled up our roster of maids and scrolled through their headshots. They were all hot...that was a requirement of the job. But none of them were calling to me. Until I saw Maeve.

When did we get a ginger on our staff?

I clicked on her picture and her file popped up.

Apparently we'd hired her a few weeks ago, which explained why I hadn't seen her. I'd hardly been in the office these past few weeks, and even if I had been, a new maid wouldn't have been assigned to the top floors. Too many sensitive documents up here to let some new girl walk around by herself. Especially with our rivals gunning for us...

I clinched my hands into fists and refocused on Maeve's file.

Twenty-two years old. Five foot six. Double D tits.

Sounds good to me.

I hit the intercom to talk to my assistant. "Send Maeve up."

"Yes, sir."

I drummed my fingers against the desk while I waited for Maeve to arrive. The girls' escape kept replaying in my head. I shouldn't have given them a ten second head start. What the hell had I been thinking?

I ran my hand through my hair and took a deep breath.

There was a light knock on my office door.

"Come in," I called and hit a button to unlock it.

Maeve walked in. She looked fucking fantastic in her maid outfit. But I was more focused on her red hair pulled into a bun behind her little black and white maid hat.

"You called, sir?" she asked in a sexy Irish accent.

Well that's a fun surprise.

I considered ordering her to get on her knees. But Ash hadn't been dressed in a maid outfit. She'd been in a bikini. And if I was gonna fuck Maeve to get Ash out of my system, I had to make her look as similar as possible.

"Pleasure to meet you," I said. "I've heard good things about you from your manager."

"Thank you, sir," she said with a shy smile and a little curtsy.

"How do you like it here so far?"

"I love it. Everyone is so nice. And the building…it's amazing. I'm actually hoping to have my wedding here. My boyfriend just proposed!" She held up her hand to show off a tiny engagement ring.

"Ah, I see what's going on here. You took a job here so that you could use your employee discount on your wedding reception." I stared at her.

"Um, uh…" She looked around nervously. "No. I mean, sure…it's a nice perk. But I also really wanted the job. I promise I'm not just going to quit right after my wedding."

I waved my hand through the air. "It's fine. Girls apply here all the time just to get a reception discount. We're used to it. As long as you do your job, it's not a problem."

"I promise I'll do great. I actually want to open my own hotel someday, so I plan on staying for quite some time and learning as much as I possibly can."

I nodded as I plotted my next move. Now that I knew she had a fiancé, I needed to come at this with a bit more finesse.

"Did you need anything else, sir?" she asked.

"I do, actually." *How can I get her in a bikini?* There were racks and racks of skimpy little bikinis for the sex auction tonight. The girls are going to strut out onto a runway as if they were fashion models, and then… *That's it!* "The real reason I called you up here is because I have a bit of an odd request. We're hosting a fashion show tonight, and one of the models is a redhead. I can't decide which color will look best with red hair, so I was hoping you could try on a few of the outfits. The model is running a little late."

"Oh wow. Well, I'm not much of a model…"

"I beg to differ. In fact, if the model doesn't show, you should walk in her place."

Maeve smiled but looked away. A few strands of hair fell over her freckled face.

God, she was just as shy as Ash. These redheads were driving me insane today.

"The changing room is just down that hallway," I said. "Third door on the left. There's a whole rack labeled V. Pick whichever one you think will look best with your red hair."

She nodded and walked off down the hall.

I started picturing her in some of the different options. Actually, I was picturing Ash in them. They were all similar to the bikini she'd worn this morning. But better.

I couldn't fucking wait to see Ash in one of them tonight.

As long as my guards can catch her.

I glanced down at the security footage on my computer and cycled through all the different cameras. I was half way through when my intercom buzzed.

"Benedict Morgan on line two," said my assistant.

It's about time that fucker called me back. Who gets a call saying that their daughter has been kidnapped and doesn't respond for two hours?

"About time you called," I said.

"Good afternoon, Magnus," replied Benedict. "Apologies for not getting back to you sooner. I was out on a rather invigorating duck hunt. Have you been hunting recently?"

"No. I don't duck hunt."

"You and Luigi should come next time."

"Go fuck yourself."

"If you can't afford to come hunting, it can be my treat. Rumor has it that the Locatelli finances have hit a bit of a rough patch."

How the hell does he know that? "Our finances are fine."

"Is that why you kidnapped one of Chastity's friends and tried to shake me down for five million dollars earlier this morning?"

"Listen up, asshole. Chastity came to save her, so now I have her too. And if you don't send me ten million dollars in the next hour, I'm gonna auction her body to the highest bidder."

"Okay."

Well that was easy. "Good. I'll text you the account number."

"Oh, no. You misunderstood. I meant that it was okay if you auction her. Chastity loves that sort of thing. I hope you gathered a nice group of suitors for her. She'll be devastated if she goes for anything less than seven figures. In fact, if the winning bid is less than a million, make it show up as a million. I'll cover the difference."

Damn it! I'd known Chastity was a freak when she let me fuck her on stage during that banana party. But I hadn't realized that Benedict was okay with her freakiness. "What kind of father are you?"

"The proudest."

"So you'd just sit back and let me sell Chastity to the highest bidder?"

"Yes. Absolutely."

"Then maybe I'll just kill her instead."

"Now, now, Magnus. I love a good kidnapping as much as the next guy, but threatening violence against my daughter is out of bounds. Unless you'd like me to send the Serbian to pay your sister a visit? I hear Idaho is lovely this time of year."

How the fuck did he find out about my sister? "I don't have a sister."

"You do. But I suppose you won't anymore if you harm a single hair on Chastity's head. Do we have an understanding?"

I clenched my fists. "You're a real dick, you know that?"

"Excellent. I really must be going, but first I'll give you a bit of advice. Chastity gets what she wants. *Always*. So if you really have captured her, then it's only because she let you do it."

"Why would she let me capture her?"

"No idea. Anyway, give your boss my very best. And my duck hunting invitation still stands." He blew a kiss into the phone and hung up.

I slammed the phone against the receiver. *Shit, shit, shit!* Why did Benedict have to be such an asshole? If he would have just paid me the ransom like a normal father, I could have called off the sex auction. And then Ash's virginity would have been all mine.

I heard heels clicking down the hall and took a deep breath.

Everything was going to be fine.

I was going to fuck Maeve and make this never-ending erection go away. And then I could stop thinking about Ash. And the sex auction would make the $5 million we needed to stay in business. For a little while, at least.

Maeve poked her head around the corner of the hallway. "I'm not sure this fits me."

"It was designed for a different model, so it's fine if it doesn't fit perfectly. It's mainly about the color. Come on out."

"Are you sure? It's a little…inappropriate."

Yes please. "I won't hold it against you." I waved her in.

She swallowed hard and then slowly walked in.

Dear Lord.

The cut of the bikini bottoms made her legs look so fucking long. But the real showstopper was the way her red hair cascaded over her massive tits. The little white top could barely contain them.

If I hadn't already had a raging boner, I would have now.

Most guys never would have been able to stand up in such a situation without totally tenting their pants. But I wasn't most guys. In my teens I'd destroyed so many pairs of pants just by getting hard. The seams just weren't strong enough. So now I had all my pants custom tailored to accommodate my foot-long cock. They had a little sleeve down one leg that I could tuck it into, which kept is secure even when erect. It was quite a brilliant design.

I made sure my cock was in its sleeve and then walked over to Maeve.

"I think it fits perfectly," I said.

"Do you like the white?" she asked.

"I can hardly see the color under your hair." I gently pushed half her hair over her shoulder, tracing my fingers over her collarbone. Her skin was so fucking soft.

She reached up and tugged on the fabric of her top, but it did nothing to cover more of her tits. If anything it just made them jiggle a bit.

Did she do that on purpose? I could have sworn she gave me a sly smile as she did it.

"I love the white. It really makes your skin look tan. And your red hair pops against it." I took a step back and raised her hand to make her do a little twirl. And her ass... *Jesus.* It was mostly hidden by her semi-sheer sarong, but I could still see the beautiful curves. "You know, after seeing this, I'm thinking I may just call and tell the other model not to come."

She tried to hide her smile as she looked up at me. But the blush on her cheeks betrayed her. She was loving this.

But then a clinging noise ruined the moment.

We both looked down at the floor and saw her engagement ring bouncing on the tile.

"Oops," she muttered. She started to bend down to pick it up, but I beat her to it.

I grabbed her hand and slid it back onto her finger. "You better get that resized," I said.

"It fits," she said. "I just sometimes play with it when I get nervous."

"Do I make you nervous, Maeve?" I asked.

"Of course you make me nervous. You're my boss. And I've heard things…"

"What have you heard?"

"That you have a short temper. And a really long…" She glanced down at my crotch. "…work day. Which is making me nervous, because my shift ended a few minutes ago. And my fiancé is picking me up. He's probably down there right now. And I don't want to keep him waiting. So I should probably go." She took a step back.

But there was no way I was letting her go. She even rambled like Ash did when she got nervous. You should have heard her on the helicopter ride right after the kidnapping. She'd told me all of her most embarrassing moments. Or at least, some of them. The list seemed *very* long.

Just like my "work day."

Nice cover-up, Maeve. But I wasn't buying it. She'd definitely heard rumors about my huge cock. And I knew she wanted a taste. I just had to keep her here a bit longer.

"You can go in just a minute," I said. "But you forgot all the accessories. Didn't you see the matching gloves and the jewelry?"

"The choker? And earrings? And the diamond studded gloves? I was scared to touch those. They looked way too expensive."

"Don't be scared," I said. "Everything is insured." It wasn't. But most of the jewels were stolen, so that made them significantly cheaper. "I know you're in a hurry, but it would be so amazing if you could run and put those accessories on. And then meet me out by the pool. I want to make see how it all sparkles in natural lighting too." I'd spent most of my time with Ash by the pool, so that was where I needed to get her out of my system.

I gave her directions from the changing room to the pool and then watched her ass jiggle as she walked out of my office.

I couldn't wait to tear that sarong off of her so that I could see the real thing.

Or...*almost* the real thing. The REAL ass I wanted belonged to Ash.

Before going out to the pool, I called down to the front desk. "Any sign of the girls?" I asked.

"None yet, sir," replied the receptionist.

"And you haven't noticed anything out of the ordinary? No strange vehicles?"

"No. Well, there was one car that kept circling the block. But it turns out he's just here to pick up one of the maids."

"Which one?"

"Maeve."

"Did you check his ID?"

"Yeah, we ran it. He's clean."

"Next time he circles around, give him a parking space and tell him that Maeve will be down in a minute." *After I'm done with her.*

I hung up and headed for the pool. But on the way out, my framed copy of the Single Boy Rules caught my eye. Specially Rule #36: Send pics and/or video to a boy if you fuck his girl. #NoSecrets.

That would be easy enough to follow. There were cameras covering every angle of the terrace. Which was good, because the look on her face when I whipped my cock out was going to be priceless. And now I'd have it on video forever.

Thank you, Single Boy Rules.

They never failed me. So I scanned them from the start to see if any other ones applied to my current situation.

Single Boy Rule #1: Friends are important, but women are queens.

Done. The diamonds that Maeve was putting on were fit for a queen.

Single Boy Rule #2: Boys' brunch is every Sunday. No exceptions.

Also done. I'd had a lovely brunch this morning with some of the high rollers who had arrived early. Honestly, leaving for that was probably the only thing that had prevented me from losing control and fucking Ash. So that was another win for the SBR.

Single Boy Rule #3: Never let your date pay for her dinner.

Of course. I wasn't going to make Maeve pay to eat my cock for dinner. That would be very rude.

Single Boy Rule #4: You can never buy her too many flowers.

Good advice. I'd have some flowers waiting for Maeve at her locker in the morning.

Single Boy Rule #5: Have cold water in your fridge at all times. Hydration is key.

Even better advice. I was pretty sure my body had been producing semen for two hours straight, so I definitely could use some water. I grabbed a few bottles out of my mini-fridge and went back to the rules.

And this time I skipped back to the section about girl-friends, starting with Rule #31: A size contest is the proper way to determine dibs on a girl.

Son of a bitch!

I'd been so horny that I'd forgotten one of the most important Single Boy Rules.

I ran over to my phone and called the front desk again.

"Is Maeve's fiancé still waiting?" I asked.

"Yes, sir."

"Excellent. Have him escorted up to my pool."

Chapter 19

CLASSIC SIZE CONTEST

The events of Sunday, Sept 22, 2013, as told by the
banana king

Maeve's fiancé got to the pool before she did.

I walked over and shook his hand. "Magnus King. Pleasure to meet you."

"Anthony Mendoza." He squeezed my hand super hard.

I cocked an eyebrow. "Impressive handshake." It wasn't. But the more confident he felt, the more likely he'd be to agree to a size contest.

"I lift a lot," he said with a shrug. "Training for my first boxing match. Anyway, where's Maeve?" He looked around the terrace.

"She'll be out in a minute. She just had to change. So what do you think of this view?"

"It's incredible."

"Maeve told me that you're thinking about having your wedding here at the Locatelli Resort and Spa. How would you like to have it up here?"

Anthony looked surprised. "Is that even an option? I don't think I saw that on the website."

"I own this place, so if I say it's an option, then it's an option."

"For real?"

"Yeah. My pleasure. Maeve has been doing a great job. And I like to take care of my employees."

"Rock on." He gave me a fist bump.

And then Maeve walked out.

Anthony's jaw dropped.

Which was reasonable. She'd looked damn good before. But now she was a fucking miracle. At first my eyes were drawn to the leash dangling between her tits. But then her sarong shifted and the sun caught some of the diamonds on the garter around her thigh. *Fuck me.* I'd forgotten the garter. But now it was all I could focus on. I couldn't wait to tear it off of her with my teeth.

"Babe!" said Maeve and ran over to Anthony. She gave him a big hug. "How'd you get up here?"

"I invited him up," I said. "The front desk said he was circling the block. And it was my fault that you were running late, so I figured he could wait up here."

"Aw, that was so nice of you."

I shrugged. "No problem."

"What are you wearing?" asked Anthony. There was a hint of anger in his voice.

"Oh. Right." She blushed. "I was just trying on some outfits for Mr. King. He has a fashion show tonight and one of his models was running late. He wanted to see what looked good with red hair." She raised her gloved hands and pushed her hair off her breasts.

"Whoa, babe!" Anthony put his hands in front of her cleavage. "Cover that up."

"The white looks amazing with her hair, right?" I asked, staring right at her tits. "And do a little spin for him to show off the back."

She did a spin.

From behind I really could just pretend she was Ash. *Perfect.*

"No," said Anthony, turning her back in the other direction. "Don't do a spin. That little skirt is see-through." He grabbed a towel off a table and wrapped it around her. "I think we should go."

That wasn't an option. I needed to get Ash out of my system or I wouldn't be able to focus on tonight. And tonight was very important. "But don't you want a tour?" I asked. I turned to Maeve. "While you were changing I was telling Anthony that you guys could have your wedding up here."

"Really?" she asked. She looked so excited.

I nodded.

"That's amazing. But how much would that cost?"

"I'd let you do it for free."

"Ah!" she squealed. "Are you serious?"

"Yup. I just need one more quick favor for the fashion show tonight."

Maeve nodded. "Anything."

Anything? "Excellent! So before I tell you what it is, I have a confession."

They both stared at me.

"I haven't been *completely* honest about what's happening tonight. Yes, there will be a fashion show. But it's actually a bit more than that. It's a sex auction."

Maeve's eyes got wide.

"I don't like the sound of this," said Anthony.

"Don't worry," I said. "I'm not asking to auction Maeve. But I do need to test out the outfit she's wearing to make sure it can hold up to the…rigors of the evening. That's actually why I invited you up here." I pointed to Anthony. "I know it's a bit awkward, and I totally understand if you guys are waiting until marriage. But it would be so helpful if you two could have sex real quick."

Maeve's eyes got even wider.

"While you watch?" asked Anthony.

I nodded. "Just to make sure her bikini doesn't rip. I'll just call out some positions for you to try, and then we'll be done. And then you can have the wedding of your dreams up here, all expenses paid." I motioned around to my beautiful terrace.

Maeve stared at me. And then she burst out laughing.

"I'm serious," I said. "I have a lot riding on this auction. I need to make sure every detail is perfect. Otherwise I would never make such a request."

"What do you think?" asked Anthony.

"I don't know…" said Maeve.

"I think we should do it. Think of all the money we'll save. We could buy a house *and* have the wedding of our dreams."

"But won't it be awkward that my boss has seen us fucking?"

"How many times have you seen me around the resort?" I asked.

"None. Until today."

"Exactly. I'm hardly ever here. And even if we do see each other, you'll have nothing to be embarrassed about. Everyone fucks."

"I guess I did say I would do anything…"

"Only if you're sure," I said.

She nodded. "I'm sure." And then she repeated it more confidently. "I'm sure."

I clapped my hands together. "Excellent! Okay, so Maeve, let's have you go inside and then walk out as if you're on the runway. And then we can pretend like Anthony wins the bidding."

Anthony and I both grabbed some lounge chairs and sat down while we waited for Maeve to emerge.

"Thanks again for doing this," I said.

"No problem, man. I should be thanking you. I had no idea how I was going to afford this wedding. And that outfit…" He whistled and shook his head.

The terrace door slid open and Maeve strutted out. I didn't know where she learned to walk a runway, but her walk was on point. Her hair blew in the wind and her tits bounced with each step.

Anthony gulped when she stopped at the end of the imaginary runway and tore off her sarong. Then she wrapped it around the back of his neck and pulled him towards her.

Here we go.

I slapped him on the back to encourage him to go up to her.

She ran her hands up his abs and tossed his shirt to the side. And then she shook her hips as she dropped down right in front of his crotch.

"Wait a second," I said just as she was about to undo his pants.

She stopped and stood back up.

"Did I do something wrong?" she asked.

"No, you were excellent. But I did have a thought. Does Anthony have a big dick?"

"You bet your ass I do."

I looked to Maeve and she nodded. "Biggest I've ever had. By far."

Interesting. I'd never lost a size contest. Could this be a first?

"Why do you ask?" said Anthony.

"Well, the guys that I invited to this sex auction are very well endowed. And I realized that the size of a member could affect the results of this test. Take those gloves, for example. They might perform fine while stroking a normal sized dick. But would the seams tear if one of my models tries to grab a real monster?"

"I'm plenty big," said Anthony. "You've got nothing to worry about."

"Okay, great. Sorry about that. Please continue."

Maeve started dancing on him again.

"Wait, wait, wait," I said. "I'm just really nervous about you not being big enough to do a proper test. I know that I am, though."

Anthony stared at me. "Oh hell no. I had a feeling you were trying to fuck my girl."

I put my hands up. "Not at all. How about this… You and I will have a size contest, and whoever is bigger will test out the outfit with Maeve."

"And by test the outfit, you mean fuck her. Right?"

"Well, yes. But it's not sexual. It's purely scientific. And to thank you for your help, I'll throw in free bachelor and bachelorette suites. And a weeklong honeymoon." I was probably throwing in too many perks, but I was desperate to get rid of this boner. And I knew a redhead was the only thing that would help.

"No way in hell," said Anthony.

"Are you sure?" asked Maeve. "I mean…that's a pretty great deal." She turned to me. "We get the suites and the honeymoon no matter who wins the size contest, right?"

I nodded. "Absolutely."

"Babe, we have to do it. You always talk about how you've never seen anyone bigger than you."

"I haven't."

"Then why not take the free stuff? What's there to be afraid of?"

"You getting fucked by him."

"But that's so unlikely. It feels like a solid gamble. And if it happens…I'm sure you'll get over it. I got over you fucking your ex a few years ago."

Oh shit.

Anthony sighed. "Okay. If you're sure…"

"I'm sure."

"Then let's do it." He turned to me. "Free wedding, free suites, and free honeymoon, right?"

"Yup." I reached out and shook his hand. "May the biggest man win. Since she's your girl, you can go first. Maeve, you have thirty seconds to bring him to full mast."

I set a timer on my watch and then went inside to grab a ruler.

Maeve was bent over and kissing down his abs when I returned. But I was more focused on the beautiful view of her ass. I couldn't wait to slide that thong off and taste her delicious pussy.

"Time's up," I said when my timer went off. "Let's see what you're working with."

Maeve dropped to her knees and took Anthony's pants with her. His erection popped up.

"Damn," I said. "You were serious about being big."

"Sorry, bud," he said with a cocky grin. "I tried to warn you. But thanks for all the free stuff."

"The game isn't over yet. We still need an official measurement." I handed Maeve the ruler.

She held it up to his length. "Eight and a quarter."

"Very impressive," I said. "My turn. Maeve, would you like to do the honors?"

She reached over and unbuttoned my pants. She was about to yank them down, but I put my hand on hers to stop her. I looked over at Anthony. "You sure you wanna risk this? We can still go back to the original deal."

"Nice try. But you can't fool me. Maeve, go ahead."

She tugged on my waistband and my cock whipped out of its sleeve and hit her right in the chin.

"Oh my God," she said with a laugh. She put her hand over her open mouth.

"What the fuck?" muttered Anthony.

I looked down at my enormous penis. Yes, Anthony was packing. Hell, he was even big enough to be a guard here at my resort. But unfortunately for him, I was the fucking king.

"I guess that means I win," I said as Maeve wrapped her luscious lips around my cock. *Fuck that feels good.*

"Jesus, Maeve," said Anthony. "Aren't you at least going to measure?"

She laughed on my cock and then pulled back and wiped her mouth. "What's there to measure?" she asked. "He's clearly bigger. This thing is like the size of my arm." She held her gloved arm up next to my cock to illustrate her point.

"Okay, fine. He's slightly bigger. That doesn't mean you had to jam it down your throat."

"I didn't jam it down my throat. Hell, I don't even know if I *could* jam it down my throat." She looked back at it. And then she opened wide and tried to go all the way down. I let out a groan as my tip pressed against her throat. But she was barely halfway. She gagged and pulled back. And I couldn't help but wonder if Ash would have taken me into her throat. I knew she was a good girl. She'd probably do exactly what she was told. The thought just made me even harder.

"Damn," she said. "Usually I can get all the way down so easily."

Sick burn.

Anthony glared at her, but she ignored him and tried to deepthroat me again.

She got a little farther this time. Until Anthony grabbed her leash and tugged her back.

"What the hell?" she said.

"Sorry," he said. "Just testing the equipment."

"Good idea," she said. "But that doesn't belong to you." She yanked the leash out of his grip and handed it to me. "So how should we test this?"

"Let's start with a fast-paced blowjob. Anthony, can you keep an eye on her tits? I want to see how secure that top is."

Maeve immediately got back to sucking. And she took my request seriously. Her long red hair was flying everywhere as her head bobbed up and down on me. And it was so easy to picture Ash in her place.

I reached down and sunk my fingers into her thick red hair, gently pressing to increase her pace. I closed my eyes, imagining Ash's lips around me.

"Dude, don't fuck her face," said Anthony.

"I'm not. *This* is fucking her face." I wrapped the leash around my hand until it was taut, and then I yanked towards myself. My cock slammed into the back of Maeve's throat. She gagged, but she also got a lot farther down than before. More importantly, she didn't try to pull back. So I gave her a little slack, and then I pulled her forward again. And again. And again.

"Come on, man. Cut that shit out."

I let her leash go slack, but she just kept the same pace. And then she leaned forward and spread her legs. The angle let her go even faster and deeper.

Fuck she's good.

Was Ash this good at giving head? I'd seen the footage of her blowing strippers at my banana party and her technique looked decent. But she also hadn't been sucking on a cock as big as mine. I pictured Ash's plump lips on my shaft instead. I had a feeling she'd just be greedy for more. Letting me teach her exactly what I liked.

I cleared my throat, trying not to forget about the ploy that got me into this position. "How are her tits looking?" I asked. "Still covered?"

"Yeah," said Anthony.

But then Maeve shook her head no and reached up and pulled her tits out. She started squeezing them as she continued to suck me off. And then she trailed her hands down her stomach and into her bikini bottoms.

"Oh God," she moaned as she touched her pussy.

Fuck me.

"You're a lucky man," I said to Anthony. "I've gotten a ton of blowjobs, but this is definitely top 5."

She slammed down on my cock.

I threw my head back in pleasure. "Maybe top 3." Especially when I wasn't looking at her. Because Ash was all I wanted. And I wanted her to suck my cock just like this.

"Okay," said Anthony. "I think that's enough of that. Can we move this along?"

"As you wish. But first can you grab me one of those waters?" I gestured to the nice cold water bottles I'd brought out. "Maeve might need one too. She's really working hard down there."

"Fuck you."

Maeve pulled back for just a second. "Babe, please. I'm so thirsty."

Anthony glared at us. And then he got us waters.

"Thanks, man," I said as he handed me the bottle. I gave him a fist bump and then took a sip while Maeve kept sucking me.

"Don't you want your water?" asked Anthony, tapping the bottle against her shoulder.

I put my hand out to stop him. "She's busy."

"But she said she was thirsty."

"I'll give her a drink." I grabbed the top of her head and tilted it back so that she was staring up at me as I stroked myself with one hand. "Open wide."

"Oh hell no," said Anthony.

It was tempting to unleash all over her face. But instead I poured water onto the tip of my cock and let it flow into her eager mouth. She caught as much as she could until it splashed out onto her chin and all over her tits.

She laughed and turned away.

"Don't laugh," said Anthony. "I thought he was about to cum on your face."

"I did too," said Maeve.

"And you kept your mouth open like that?"

"I'm just trying to do a good job. How'd my outfit hold up?" she asked, looking down at her bikini. She blushed when she noticed her tits were out of her top. Even though she was the one who'd taken them out.

That was definitely something Ash would do. Which made me dick stiffen even more.

"So far so good," I said. "Now, let's see about this thong…" I helped her to her feet, grabbed both sides of her thong, and pulled in either direction. It easily tore in half.

Maeve let out a gasp. And she let out a bigger gasp when I knelt down, hitched one of her legs over my shoulder, and started licking her delicious pussy.

She was already fucking soaked, and not just from the water I'd poured on her. I squeezed her firm ass and let my tongue explore deeper. And then I effortlessly picked her up and lay her back on the bar.

I didn't even have to push on her thighs to spread her legs. She did it for me. And then she grabbed my hair and pulled me down.

I was used to being in control, but I loved when girls showed me what they wanted. And I was more than happy to give it to her. I closed my eyes, imagining Ash's fingers buried in my hair. Her whimpering every time I swirled my tongue around her wetness. Randomly shouting out her greatest fears as she lost control. Soon my dick ripping her in half would be added to that list.

I feasted until Ash's entire body shook, her thighs clasping around my head. *Fuck. No. Maeve's thighs. Not Ash's.* This was supposed to be helping, but still all I could think about was Ash.

"Oh fuck," Maeve moaned.

"What the fuck, babe?" said Anthony. "Did you just come?"

"No," she lied. "Maybe."

"How is this even testing the outfit?" he asked. "Your top is barely on and he tore the bottoms."

Fair point. And this wasn't helping my current predicament. I needed to fuck her. So I could picture my cock spreading Ash's pussy wide. I wanted every inch of me slick with her juices.

I gave Maeve a few more licks and then stood up. "It's not," I said. "But did you really want me to fuck her with this without properly warming her up?" I pointed to my huge cock.

Anthony glared at me.

"So what position should we test first?" I asked.

"How about doggy?" suggested Maeve.

"What the hell? You never ask for doggy."

"I just thought it was the best one to test." She bent over and grabbed the bar. "We need to see if the bikini strap can withstand being used for leverage to fuck my brains out."

"Wouldn't using the leash make more sense?" asked Anthony.

"Good idea," I said. "I'll test both."

"Fuck," muttered Anthony.

"Don't worry, man. I know it's awkward to watch another guy fuck your girl. But with this position she can look into your eyes the whole time. So it'll basically be like it's you fucking her, just with a much bigger cock." I slapped my cock against Maeve's ass. "Ready for this?"

"Yes," she said without missing a beat.

"Anthony?" I asked.

"Just get it over with," he said.

"Okay. Here we go…" It was tempting to slam into her. To feel her tight pussy stretching around my thick cock. But I wanted to savor this moment. I'd been dreaming of fucking Ash all morning.

And this was almost as good as the real thing.

I ran my hand along her soft freckled skin, tracing the curve of her hips.

I'd never been so fucking hard in my life.

I wrapped her leash around my hand to get it nice and tight. And then I grabbed my cock and got ready to guide it into her.

Your virgin pussy is mine, Ash.

Interlude

SO MANY QUESTIONS
Saturday - Oct 10, 2026

Ash hit pause on the recording. It was a beautiful close-up of the banana king's throbbing cock about a centimeter away from claiming Maeve.

"Oooh, nice timing," I said and took a screenshot. "Now shall we continue?"

"I have so many questions."

"Can they wait until after? Because we were *just* getting to the good part. I mean…the whole thing is a good part, really. Like when he poured water into her mouth…" I fanned myself. "Sign me up, Daddy."

"Your daddy did kind of sign you up for that in a way… I mean, you heard what he said on that call. He wanted you to get auctioned."

"Right? Best daddy ever! Speaking of which…I can't wait for him to walk me down the aisle. And speaking of walking down aisles…we should really get back to this video." I reached to hit play, but Ash blocked me.

"What do aisles have to do with this video? Is that a reference to Maeve and Anthony planning on having their wedding up there?"

"Is that your only question? If so, we should just roll the tape and you'll get your answer."

"No, I have other questions."

"Such as?"

"Well first and foremost, why do you have this video? And why are we watching it? And was it really appropriate for the banana king to splice in the security footage from the terrace?"

"I think it was very thoughtful of him. I mean look at that dick." I grabbed my phone and zoomed in even more for her.

"Right. But isn't this a report he submitted to his boss?"

I nodded. "Sure is. I, for one, appreciate his thoroughness. Good work is hard to find these days."

Ash shrugged. "Fair point. But seriously…why are we watching this part? Can't we just fast forward to the sex auction?"

"Who said anything about a sex auction?"

"That's literally what this entire story has been about!" She pointed at the video. "My virginity is about to be auctioned off and I'm freaking dying over here trying to figure out who took it."

"I mean…it's really looking like the banana king might lose control and claim your virgin pussy." I wiggled my eyebrows at her. "Isn't it so hot how much he wants you? You're a lucky girl."

"So he *does* take it?"

I shrugged.

"Gah! Can you pleeeeease just tell me?"

I shook my head. "No can do. Like Uncle Mortimer always used to say, learning who took one's virginity is one of those things that should only be seen and not heard."

Ash looked confused. "I thought that was a Victorian school boy in a drawing room?"

"Whoa, what? You think a Victorian school boy took your virginity in a drawing room? Or are you saying that a

Victorian school boy in a drawing room was the one who gave that sage advice rather than Uncle Mortimer?"

"Neither. I was saying that Victorian school boys should be seen and not heard."

"Rude."

"Never mind! We're really getting off topic here…"

"We really are," I said with a laugh. "Let's get back to it. And before you ask again to fast forward…the answer is no way. Because this next part may or may not have been my primary inspiration for my wedding ceremony. Spoiler alert: It was." I winked at her and hit play.

Chapter 20

CAUGHT RED HANDED

The events of Sunday, Sept 22, 2013, as told by the
banana king

The terrace door opened just as I was about to claim Maeve.

Damn it.

Five guards walked onto the terrace.

"Sir," said the squad leader with a salute.

"Give me good news," I snapped. If they'd interrupted this for nothing, I would fire every single one of their asses.

The squad leader nodded. "With pleasure, sir. Bravo Squad has located the girls."

Fucking finally! "Where are they?"

"In the bachelorette suite. They were pretending to be bridesmaids, and apparently they put on a *very* convincing performance."

"Clever little sluts. Wait… No one fucked the redhead, did they?" I looked down at my own redhead.

Was it fate that I hadn't fucked Maeve yet? Was this never-ending erection destined to end up in Ash?

No. I couldn't have Ash. Because we needed to auction her virginity and get five million fucking dollars.

The squad leader shook his head. "She sucked a lot of dicks, but no one fucked her."

"Good. Let's bring them up to the dressing room and get them prepped for the auction."

"Roger that."

"I guess that means this size contest is officially over," said Anthony. He held his hand out for Maeve.

"Size contest?" asked the squad leader. "Mind if we measure in?"

Yes. I minded very much. But it would have been very poor etiquette to deny his request. "Sure thing."

"Measure in?" asked Anthony and Maeve at the same time.

"Yeah. If they're bigger than you, they get to join."

Anthony shook his head. "Hell no."

"You can't really say no. Single Boy Rule #24: If a boy interrupts a size contest, you must let him measure in." As always, I realized that the Single Boy Rules were right again. If I didn't let Maeve warm up with a smaller cock, I might have torn the poor girl in two.

Anthony laughed. But when we all just stared at him, he cleared his throat. "Wait, you're serious?"

I nodded. "Yup. But I'll tell you what. I just got some great news, so I'm feeling generous. And this whole thing is about your wedding venue. So if you want, we can settle this with a classic Uskavian wedding ceremony."

"Uskavian?"

"Yeah. From the Kingdom of Uskavia. Very small country. Most people don't even know about it. But you don't need a geography lesson. What's important is their wedding ceremony. It's pretty traditional, but the twist is that the bride measures all the groomsmen. And if at least half of them are bigger than the groom, then they get to fuck her. In our little mock wedding, these five guards will be your groomsmen."

"So if I'm bigger than at least three of them, we're done?" asked Anthony.

"Correct." I turned to Maeve. "Also, if Anthony loses, you'll be my personal maid until your wedding day. Which, to be clear, means I'll fuck you whenever I please."

Maeve gulped.

"So what do you say?"

"Let's do it."

"What?" asked Anthony. "You're seriously considering this?"

"Would you rather me get impaled by that?" She gestured to my huge cock. "This is our way out. You got unlucky with Mr. King. The odds of three of those guards being bigger than you are basically zero."

"We have a deal?" I asked.

"Yup." Maeve shook my hand. "Set it up."

Done.

I got dressed while the guards gathered some furniture and flowers to make it feel wedding-y. Meanwhile, Maeve grabbed her sarong and ducked into a bathroom to fix her wedding look.

In just under two minutes, all the guys were standing on the altar – me at the center, Anthony on my left, and the five guards next to him as his groomsmen.

The squad leader hit a button on his phone and wedding music started playing.

Maeve walked out of the bathroom. All she'd done for her wedding dress was wrapped her sheer sarong around her waist and pulled her bikini top back into place.

And honestly…it kind of worked. The only thing weird about it was that the sarong tied in the front, so it left her pussy exposed. So it looked imbalanced with her tits covered.

She must have agreed with me, because she took one step, looked in the mirror, and then pushed her top off her tits.

Good girl.

"Why'd you take your tits out?" whispered Anthony when she got to the altar.

"It looks weird to have them covered when my cooch is out. And anyway…when you win, it'll just make your groomsmen that much more jealous that I'm all yours." She squeezed his hands and then took her place across from him at the altar.

"Dearly beloved," I began. "We gather here today to celebrate the love that Anthony and Maeve share for one another. And to see if Anthony has a bigger dick than his groomsmen. Earlier he measured in at eight and a quarter, so that's the baseline. Maeve, would you like to do the honors?" I handed her the ruler.

She smiled at me. "It would be my pleasure." She walked to the end of the line and undid one of the guard's pants.

I took a deep breath. I honestly didn't know how big these five guys were. We had a minimum hiring requirement of eight inches, but a lot of our guards measured in right around that mark. So this could easily go Anthony's way.

Maeve tugged on the guard's pants and his cock popped out.

Damn. This one was gonna be close.

She held the ruler up to him and…

"Eight and one eighth," she said.

"One point for Anthony," I said.

He let out a sigh and nodded as she moved to the next guard. Who was…tiny.

Like, super tiny.

Maeve laughed and Anthony gave a big fist pump in the air.

"What the hell is that?" I asked.

"Three inches," said Maeve through her laughter.

"Give me a minute…" muttered the guard. But he wasn't fooling anyone. He was a rock hard three inches.

I shook my head. "You're fired. Give me your badge and see yourself out."

He pulled his pants back up and moped off the terrace.

I felt for him, but he had no business wearing a Locatelli Resort and Spa uniform. I'd have to look into our hiring practices and see how he'd slipped through the cracks.

"Anthony is up two to zero," I said. "If this next one is smaller than eight and a quarter, then Anthony wins."

Maeve went to the next guard. As she knelt in front of him, he dropped his pants. His cock swung out and bounced against her tits.

"Ah!" she yelped.

"What's that noise for?" I asked. "Excited?"

"Surprised. I wasn't expecting him to be black."

"You ever been with a black guy before?"

She shook her head.

"Well, there's a first time for everything. What's his size?"

She grabbed it and measured it.

"Whoa, babe," said Anthony. "Don't touch another dick."

"I had to in order to measure. It's too heavy to stand up on its own. Which makes sense, because it's nine inches."

Fuck yeah! "Alright. Two for Anthony, one for the groomsmen. Is the comeback on?"

"No way," said Anthony.

Maeve went to the fourth guard and gasped when his cock flung out.

"I know you," she muttered.

"What?" asked Anthony. "You've seen his cock before?"

"It's nothing bad, babe. On my first day I just accidentally walked into the men's shower and saw..." she pointed to the huge cock in front of her. "I only recognize it because of the big heart-shaped birthmark."

That checked out. Most of his cock was dark black, but one splotch was much lighter.

"Don't worry," said the guard through his voice modulator. "Nothing happened. Although I admit, I have been dreaming of burying my face in those tits ever since." He reached out and honked one of Maeve's breasts.

Maeve swatted him away. "Hey! Hands off. Unless this next guy is bigger. Then I guess you're allowed to put your hands wherever you want to."

"Wait, he saw your tits?"

Maeve nodded. "Well...yeah. I was going in there to take a shower so I was naked."

Anthony shook his head.

"How big is he?" I asked. But I didn't really need to. He was way bigger than Anthony.

Maeve grabbed him to measure. "Eleven and a quarter."

"Okay," I said. "It all comes down to this. If the best man is smaller than you, than you win. But if he's bigger...then Maeve is gonna get *fucked*."

"Ready, babe?" asked Maeve.

Anthony nodded.

Maeve dropped the groomsman's pants and...

It was gonna be close.

She put the ruler up to it. It was right around eight inches. But then she pushed the ruler into the skin at the base of his cock. "Eight and three eighths," she said.

Oh damn! She'd definitely made it so that the groomsmen would win. That naughty little slut.

"Fuck," groaned Anthony.

"Gentleman," I said. "You may fuck the bride."

They were on her in a second.

The guy with the birthmark tore off his gloves and went straight for her tits. The nine-incher came up behind her and tore her sarong off.

And the best man started fingering her pussy. He groaned. "She's so wet for us."

Maeve turned so red and gave a nervous laugh. And then her laugh turned into a moan when the guy behind her slapped her ass.

"Hey," said Anthony. "Don't hit her."

"It's okay, babe," said Maeve. "I kind of like it. Getting spanked. Not getting touched by three hot guys all at once. I'm not enjoying this at all." She did not sound very convincing.

"So which cock did you want to not-enjoy first?" I asked.

"Hmmm…" Maeve took a step back from the men and looked down at their cocks.

First she walked over to the nine-incher and unbuckled his vest. She pushed it off his shoulders and then trailed her hands down his eight-pack. But she stopped just short of his cock.

She walked to the best man next.

"It's best to start with me," he said. "I'm the closest in size to your boyfriend, so it'll be an easy transition for you."

"Good point," she said and stroked his cock. She started to drop to her knees, but then she popped back up and let go of him.

And then she was on her knees in front of the final guy. The one with the birthmark. And his cock was down her throat.

"Looks like she's made her choice," I said.

She nodded on his cock.

"Seriously?" asked Anthony. "You chose the biggest one?"

She got back up. "I just thought it would be less awkward since I already know him. It's so naughty to just bend over and let a complete stranger fuck me. And anyway, he's the second biggest. Mr. King is still going to fuck me, right?"

I nodded. "Absolutely. I just thought it would be courteous to let the boys warm you up first."

"So thoughtful," she said and handed Birthmark her leash.

He spun her around and pushed on her back to bend her over.

Maeve's eyes got huge as he slowly slid his massive cock inside of her.

"Wait!" yelled Anthony. He ran around over and looked in horror at the huge cock half way in his fiancée's pussy.

"What's wrong?" asked Birthmark.

"Did you seriously not put a condom on?"

"No."

Anthony put his hand on his forehead. "Fuck man, I haven't even gotten to do that yet."

Oh shit.

"Well then you're in for a treat," said Birthmark. "Her pussy feels fucking fantastic." He pulled on her hips and slid into her more.

"Dude, stop!"

"Babe," said Maeve. "It's fine. I'm on birth control. And I doubt they make condoms big enough for him."

I walked over and put my arm around Anthony's shoulders. "Don't worry, it's not like he's going to cum in her. Single Boy Rule #27: Unless you're dating, always finish on her face or tits."

She arched her back and pressed against him.

"I'll try my best," said Birthmark. "But with an ass like this…no promises." He slapped her ass and slammed into her pussy.

"This is fucked up," said Anthony. "He's not even testing the outfit."

"Right," said Maeve, looking back at the guy fucking her. "You're supposed to fuck me so hard that my bikini top breaks."

"I can do that," said Birthmark. He grabbed the bikini strap across her back and increased his pace. Within a few thrusts, he was fucking her mercilessly.

Her moans got louder with every thrust.

It was just as hot as any of the banana party footage we had. And yet…I was still thinking of Ash. It was a good thing she wasn't here though, because there was no way I could have shared her.

"Harder," Maeve panted.

He pulled as far back as possible and slammed into her at full force. The bikini strap snapped and her entire body shook with pleasure.

"Fuckkkkkk," she screamed. But it was silenced half way through by the nine-incher shoving his cock down her throat. And then she started stroking the squad leader.

"Well that's interesting," I said, pointing to her glove that was starting to tear at the seams. "It appears stroking smaller cocks is actually more likely to make them rip. I would have thought the opposite, but I guess it kinda makes sense. The smaller the cock, the more she has to bend her fingers to get around it. Like on mine, her hand was basically still wide open. It's a good thing we tested this."

"Great," said Anthony. "All her clothes are ruined, so I think we're done here."

"But…" said Maeve. She looked down at her torn glove. And then at her ruined top on the ground by her feet.

"My heels could still snap. Or some of those diamonds could pop off if they put me on all fours."

"Better test it," I said.

"I agree," said Maeve. She stood up, grabbed the nine-incher, and walked him over to a lounge chair. He tossed her onto all fours and then started fucking her from behind.

"Oh fuck," she moaned. "You're all so big. I can't believe the rumors were true."

"Rumors?" asked Anthony. "You knew all the guards were huge when you agreed to have the Uskavian wedding?"

"Umm…" said Maeve. But she never had to finish her thought, because the squad leader stuck his cock in her mouth.

Damn she's a freak. Just like Ash.

I couldn't wait to claim Maeve once the guards stretched her out a bit. But I wanted to make sure that I could really picture Ash when I did it.

I reached into my pocket for my phone so I could bring up the security feed of the girls, but I'd left it in my office.

"You," I said, pointing to the first guard who had failed to measure in. "Give me your phone."

"Yes, sir." He took his phone out of one of his tactical vest pockets and tossed it to me.

I pulled up the security feed of the dressing room. But the girls weren't there yet. And they weren't in the elevator. Or in the hall outside the bachelorette suite.

Oh fuck. These idiots better not have let the girls escape again.

"Sergeant," I yelled.

But there was no response.

I looked over at the gangbang. Maeve was now straddling the squad leader on the lounge chair. He'd tossed his helmet to the side and her tits were hitting him in the face as she bounced up and down on his cock.

"Get her tits out of his face," I demanded to Birthmark.

He saluted and grabbed her leash to pull Maeve's head towards his own cock. She opened wide to suck him off. And more importantly, her tits were now out of the squad leader's face.

"Sergeant!" I yelled again.

"Yes sir?" he asked.

"Did you give the command to bring the girls up to the dressing room?"

"No, sir. We got interrupted by Anthony asking about the size contest before I could give the order."

"Damn it, Sergeant. You just lost your pussy privileges for the next five minutes. Birthmark, you're up again. And you," I said to the fifth guy. "I need your radio."

He handed it to me.

I hit the button to open the channel. "Bravo Squad, where the fuck are you?"

"In the bachelorette suite awaiting your orders," came the response. "We found the girls."

"Bring them up to the dressing room."

"Copy that."

I hung up the radio and switched my security feed to the footage of the hallway outside of the bachelorette suite. The door opened and...

Hot damn.

All three girls were completely naked, except for heels, handcuffs, and black bags over their heads. A guard stood behind each, pushing them down the hall.

My dick stiffened at the sight of Ash's red hair cascading over her beautiful breasts. I couldn't believe that some asshole was going to get to fuck her tonight.

Her virgin pussy should be mine.

And maybe it would be. She'd be in the dressing room any minute. She was handcuffed. And bagged. I could just bend her over and take what I wanted.

But then she wouldn't be a virgin anymore. And she wouldn't be worth the five million dollars we needed.

Fuck!

I needed to get rid of this boner before Ash got to the roof, or I wasn't sure I'd be able to control myself.

I took a mental snapshot of her beautiful naked body and then turned back to Maeve getting spit roasted by the guards. She definitely did *not* have a virgin pussy. But I could pretend.

"My turn," I said. "You all have thirty seconds to cum."

Birthmark kept fucking her from behind as he grabbed her leash to tilt her head up towards Nine-inches and the squad leader.

She stuck her tongue out and smiled up at them just before they unleashed all over her face.

If she hadn't been getting fucked from behind, the blast might have knocked her over. Within a second she was absolutely *covered*. Those pretty freckles? Hidden under a glaze of cum. Her beautiful tits? Dripping with it.

"What the fuck?" yelled Anthony. "Don't cum in her mouth!"

They didn't listen. They just kept cumming.

But Birthmark was much more accommodating. He saluted Anthony and then slammed into Maeve's pussy. And by the way his abs were tensing, I had a feeling he was filling her with cum.

Nine-inches aimed his final shot up into her red hair.

And then it was my turn.

I glanced back one final time at the security footage. Ash's legs looked so damned sexy as she stepped into the elevator. I switched the feed to the elevator camera just as one of the guards pressed the button for the... Lobby?

What the fuck?

I grabbed my radio. "Bravo Squad. Where the hell are you going?"

No answer.

"Bravo squad. Do you copy?"

Still no answer. And I could see on my screen that none of the guards in the elevator even grabbed their radios. They just calmly stepped off the elevator into the lobby. Towards the exit.

Fuck!

Chastity must have seduced those guards into helping her escape. Or maybe her father had planted some fake guards amongst our ranks months ago. Either way, those fuckers were about to walk all three girls right out the front door, just like Chastity had promised.

"All units, head to the lobby. Do not let them exit the building. I repeat: do *not* let the girls exit the building."

I sprinted to my personal elevator and jammed the button for the lobby.

I'd never been so thankful for the high-speed elevators we'd installed. A trip that would have usually taken 2 minutes took a little over 20 seconds.

When the doors opened, the girls were only a few feet away from the exit.

"STOP!" I yelled. My voice echoed through the lobby.

The imposter guards stopped and turned around.

"Sir?" asked the Bravo Squad sergeant. Or the one pretending to be the sergeant.

"Where the hell do you think you're going?"

"To the limo."

"What limo?"

"The one we're gonna use to drive them to the airport."

I stared at him.

"To take them to Mr. Locatelli. Like you told us to a minute ago."

"I told you to?"

"Yeah. On the radio."

"I never told you to go to the limo. I said to bring them to the dressing room." I turned to Delta Squad, who had just entered the lobby from the east hall. "Grab them."

They rushed over and grabbed the girls.

"The guards too."

Delta Squad grabbed the three Bravo Squad guards.

"Permission to speak freely?" asked a Delta guard.

"Go ahead," I said.

"I heard it too. You told Bravo Squad to take them to the limo and drive them to the airport."

What the fuck? "God damn it. When those bitches got into the control room they must have hacked our radios." I walked towards the girls and started a slow clap. "Well played, Chastity. Well played. I thought you were crazy when you told me that you were gonna walk through the front door. But you got pretty damned close. You probably can't see with those bags over your head, but you were literally three steps away from winning. But alas… You lost. And now I'm going to collect my prize."

I circled the three girls.

All three of them were fucking perfect. Chastity's tanned tits were the best I'd ever seen. And the ass on her other friend…*sweet Lord.* But my eyes kept gravitating to Ash. To her long red hair peeking out under the bag on her head. To the freckles on her chest, stopping just above her lovely breasts. To her virgin pussy.

Fuck it.

I'd figure out another way to get the five million dollars. I had to have her.

I took a step towards her.

But then I noticed that people were starting to stop and stare. One of them pulled their phone out and started filming.

Damn it.

It wasn't that I minded an audience. In fact, I preferred it. But there was no way I'd be able to convince the guys at the auction that Ash was a virgin if the nightly news was rolling video of me fucking her in my lobby.

"Sorry about this, folks," I said, pointing to the naked girls. "These three drank a little too much from the minibar and thought it would be fun to go streaking." I turned to the guards and dropped my voice to a whisper. "Take them up to the dressing room and start getting them prepped for the auction."

"Yes sir," said the Bravo sergeant.

"Not you," I said. "You three idiots almost let them get away. Get the hell out of my sight before I fire you." I gestured towards the exit.

"Sir, yes sir," he said through his voice modulator.

The three Bravo guards turned and walked out the door.

Good riddance.

As the other guards walked the girls past me to the elevator, I grabbed Ash's arm. "You've been playing games with me all day," I whispered to her. "As soon as we get upstairs, I'm gonna fuck you so hard."

Chapter 21

SABOTAGE

The events of Sunday, Sept 22, 2013, as told by the

banana king

The dick-sleeve in my pants was extremely sturdy. But it was struggling to contain my erection as I stepped off the elevator and made my way to the dressing room.

"Sir," said my assistant as I passed by her desk.

"Yes?"

"Mr. Locatelli is on line 2. He said it's urgent."

Fuck. I nodded and went into my office to take the call.

"Magnus speaking," I said into the phone.

"We have a problem."

"I took care of it. The girls are in our custody. And the buyers..." I glanced at the security footage of the pre-auction lounge. Most of the leather sofas were already occupied by buyers in masquerade masks sipping on cocktails. And there was a line out the door. "We've got a full house. I'm confident we can get the five million."

"I'm not. Your failed attempt to bribe Benedict Morgan tipped him off that we're struggling. My informants tell me that he's convinced the other families to bid low tonight. And once we go bankrupt, he's gonna buy all our property on the cheap."

"That mother fucker."

"That's not all. I just got off the phone with regulators in Italy. They're fining us three million euro for some bullshit. So now we need this auction to bring in eight million."

"That's not possible," I said. "Especially with the families colluding to bid low." I'd just had a lovely brunch with those fuckers this morning. How dare they plot behind my back.

"For your sake, I hope it's possible. You've served me well, Magnus. But I will not tolerate failure. Do I make myself clear?"

"Crystal clear."

The call ended.

Fuck! I slammed my fist against my desk.

I couldn't believe how quickly all of this was unraveling.

My Italian villa village was going to make us billions of dollars. It was going to cement our position as one of the wealthiest crime families in the world. But then Chastity's father had pulled some strings and gotten our building permits revoked, leaving us with hundreds of millions of dollars' worth of the finest Italian finishes in the world and nowhere to install them.

And now my boss was going to kill me if I couldn't earn eight million dollars at a fucking rigged sex auction.

I took a deep breath. It would be fine. I thought best under pressure.

Maybe I could just kidnap all the high rollers and ransom them back to their families.

No. Pissing off every crime family in the world was just about the worst idea I'd ever come up with. Sure, we might get the money. But then a week from now I'd be walking down the street and get a bullet in the brain.

Maybe I could…

But I had zero ideas. Every time I moved my never-ending erection rubbed against my dick sleeve. All I could think about was claiming Ash's virgin pussy.

And why shouldn't I? Earlier today, it seemed wrong to try to sell a fake virgin. But if those fuckers were going to collude to try to put us out of business, why shouldn't I sell them a fake? As long as I came on her face instead of inside of her, they'd never know the difference.

And once I got her out of my system, I'd be able to come up with a proper plan.

I stood up from my desk and went to the dressing room.

There were racks of clothes and dress forms in bikinis and jewelry displays. But what I was interested in were the seven dressing areas separated by thick black curtains.

I pulled the first curtain back.

The girl inside was putting some finishing touches on her makeup. But she wasn't Ash.

Neither were the next two.

And then I realized my mistake. She was walking last, so she was probably in the last dressing area. I walked to the other end of the room and pulled the curtain back.

Oh damn.

She was checking her ass out in the mirror. Which was odd, because her head was still covered with a bag. But this bag was white instead of black like it had been in the lobby.

I started to step through the curtain, but a man in a *very* sparkly suit pulled me back and blocked my path.

"Who the hell are you?" I asked.

"Who the hell are *you*?" he replied, giving me the up-down. He sounded very excited to see me. "Actually, don't answer that. Tonight you'll be whoever I want you to be. Because I'm in charge of this dressing room."

"I'm…"

He put his finger on my lips to silence me. "Hush, you big, beautiful beef tower."

I swatted his hand away.

"Oooh, feisty." He gave a little shimmy. "Bring that energy to the runway and you'll sell for millions."

Would I? Had this dude just given me the key to solving my eight-million-dollar predicament? No. He definitely had not. Because I was pretty sure none of the buyers in attendance tonight were gay. If I tried to sell myself I'd just be the laughing stock of the crime world.

"I'm not getting auctioned," I said.

"Not in that pant, you aren't."

"What's wrong with this pant? And why are we calling it a singular pant instead of pants?"

"You're right. Those hardly even qualify as a pant." He shook his head. "Tragic."

I usually wouldn't have been insulted by such a statement. But the savagery of the way he delivered it was devastating.

"Don't worry. I'll find you something *much* better to walk in. What size are you?"

"Uh…I think I wear a 36-34?"

"I meant your crotch size."

"Are you asking how long my dick is?"

He nodded. "How else am I going to find you a proper man-thong? We can't risk going too small and having a tip slip on the runway. Or going too big and making it look…empty. So how big is it? Seven inches? Eight inches?"

"I'm over a foot." *Why the hell did I just tell him that?*

His eyes lit up and went straight to my crotch. "I'm sorry, did I forget to introduce myself? Justin Belle, professional stylish at Odegaard Miami, and this evening's stand-in for Ernie. He called out sick at the last minute."

Ah. That explains a lot. "Magnus King," I said and shook his hand. "The owner of this resort."

"Oh my God." He put his hand over his mouth. "I'm so sorry I didn't recognize you. And the pant comment. That was totally out of line. I know it must be difficult to find a stylish pant to contain your massive member. If you want to slip out of those I can probably make a few adjustments... No! There's no time!" He took a huge gulp of coffee from the biggest, most heavily bedazzled tumbler I'd ever seen. "I promise I'll sew you a sexy little pant later, but first I need to finish these veils."

"Veils?" I asked.

"Yes." He pulled back the curtain and pointed to the white bag on Ash's head. It was roughly the same shape as the one she'd been bagged with earlier. But this one was made of expensive white fabric. And there were diamond-studded buttons up the side of it holding it together. "When I showed up and found the girls wearing nothing but heels and bags over their heads, I thought Ernie had lost the plot. But then I got to thinking..."

"Oh, those aren't supposed to be part of it. You can just take those off." I stepped towards Ash and grabbed for the bag, but Justin swatted my arm away from her. "Stop that," I said.

"You stop it. You can't take her veil off before the show. You'll ruin the reveal, you fat head."

"The reveal?"

"Yes. The most important part of any fashion show. Or sex auction."

"The buyers need to see what they're bidding on."

"I disagree. Think about it. If you ended up on a surprise date with a hot stud, would you be more intrigued if he showed up nude? Or would you rather spend all night wondering how thick that foot-long sausage is gonna be when you unwrap it after the show?" He stared at my crotch the whole time he was speaking.

"I'm not gay, so I would be intrigued by neither of those scenarios."

He sighed. "It's all about anticipation."

"I think I see what you're saying. One of my favorite parts of sex is whipping out my massive cock and seeing the look on the girl's face. Sometimes they just stare at it in shock. Or sometimes they cover their mouth and giggle." *Like Maeve did earlier.* "Or sometimes they just start sucking me immediately."

"Exactly," said Justin. "If you already knew how they'd react, it wouldn't be as fun. The same goes for a proper reveal. You never know what saucy little number you'll see when he pulls off his cape. Or in this case…your bidders won't know what kind of exotic beauty they're buying. Mystery is sexy."

Shit, he was right. Mystery was definitely sexy. That was basically what we were selling with our banana party videos. The free previews we released would always show a room full of hot girls cheering for well-endowed strippers. But if you wanted to see which girls would get on their knees, you'd have to subscribe.

And then it hit me.

The perfect fucking plan!

"You're a genius," I said. "Get those veils finished. And amp up the body contouring. These girls need to look flawless on camera."

"You got it," replied Justin, but I was already sprinting out of the dressing room back to my office.

If I was going to pull this off, I had work to do.

"Get my tuxedo ironed," I said to my assistant. "And get someone from IT into my office ASAP."

While I waited for the tech guy, I scrolled through my contacts and called the anchor of *Entertainment Miami,* Adriana Gomez.

"Hola, Magnus," she said in her sexy Latina accent. "I can't really talk right now. We're going live in twenty."

"Cancel your broadcast for tonight," I said.

"I can't just cancel the entire broadcast."

"I meant cancel what you were planning to talk about. Because I'm giving you a sneak peek at the new Odegaard swim collection."

"Hmmm…tempting. But Beyoncé literally just walked into our studio. She's giving us an exclusive live interview tonight."

Shit. "Well air it another night. I promise I'll make it up to you."

"How?"

"I have a reservation tomorrow night at that new Puerto Rican place everyone is raving about. You could be my plus one."

"I've been there three times already. You've gotta do better than that."

"Hold please." I whipped my dick out, held it next to a remote control for scale, and snapped a pic for her. Then I hit send.

Adriana sighed. "Damn it. How do you expect a girl to say no to that?"

"So we have a deal?"

"Yeah. I'll air your fashion show. But you have to take me to the Puerto Rican place too. Their mofongo is to die for."

"You would love mofongo."

"What's that supposed to mean? Are you calling me fat?"

"No. But mofongo is made of plantains. And I happen to know for a fact that you love shoving plantains down your throat." She'd hired me to throw a red-carpet-themed bachelorette party for her bestie a few months ago. Long story short, she ended up with my cock down her throat on the red carpet while her friends pretended to be paparazzi and snapped a ton of photos.

She laughed. "You're an idiot. Have your IT guys send us the live feed."

"Will do. Thanks, Adriana. I owe you one."

"No, you owe me like…four. Which is why you're gonna bring four friends to dinner."

"The reservation is for two."

"That's fine. I'm not interested in eating with them. I'm interested in fucking them." She hung up.

Oh damn. That would be quite the fun evening. If I was still alive to enjoy it.

This better go flawlessly.

Chapter 22

THE AUCTION

The events of Sunday, Sept 22, 2013, as told by the

banana king

"We're on in three, two…" The director mouthed, "one," and then pointed to me.

I adjusted my white bowtie, pulled my black and white monkey mask over my head, and strode onto the stage.

Usually the sun setting over the Miami ocean would have been visible through the three story window behind the stage. But not today. We were broadcasting this to the world. And with what we were about to do, we couldn't risk giving any hints about our location. So we'd found some stock footage of a Caribbean beach and projected that onto the windows instead.

"Gentleman," I said. And then a group of masked women in black cocktail dresses lounging in one of the cabanas caught my eye. "And ladies. It is my honor to welcome you to a very special sneak peek of the brand new Odegaard summer collection. Please enjoy."

I gave a bow and took a step back as the first model walked past me, her diamond studded gloves sparkling under the bright lights. She must have been able to see out of the bag Justin had made to cover her head, because she turned at just the right moment to hit the runway. Her heels splashed in the thin layer of water covering the glass runway as sharks circled under her.

So far, so good.

"Any buzz yet?" I asked into my earpiece. I'd instructed the control room to monitor #Odegaard on Twitter.

"Just one mention so far," replied the director. "And that was from the official *Entertainment Miami* account."

That was okay. The fun had hardly begun.

"Make sure you show shots of the buyers," I replied.

"Roger that."

The first model struck a pose at the end of the runway. One of the many camera men wearing a monkey mask ran over and got a nice-closeup of her before she turned and walked back towards me. I took her hand and helped her do a little spin.

"The bidding starts at $50,000," I said into my microphone. "Do I hear 50?"

A guy in a cabana to the left raised his paddle. I was pretty sure he was with the Russian mob.

"I have 50. Will you give me 60?"

Another paddle raised.

"Still not many mentions," said the director into my ear.

Damn.

"I have 60. Will you give me 75?" I asked.

The Russian dude bid 75. But no one would go up to 100.

"Going once, going twice. Sold to cabana #4 for $75,000! Please come get your prize." *You cheap bastard.* I'd never once sold a girl for less than 100K at one of these auctions. Luigi's informant had been spot on that they were colluding to bid low.

The Russian guy came up and I handed him her leash. He led her back to his cabana and pulled the curtains shut.

Fuck this. I wasn't going to keep selling these beautiful women for next to nothing. It was insulting to them.

"Let's go to plan B," I said into my earpiece. It was a little premature since it meant we'd make no money on the next few girls. But I was betting on this strategy paying off big at the end.

"Heard. Activating plan B."

The next model came out and did her walk. And then I started the bidding.

One of the cabanas started the bidding at $50,000. But then the guards I'd planted as fake buyers in cabanas #8, #9, and #10 took control and started bidding each other all the way up to 300K.

"Sold to cabana #8 for $300,000!" I announced.

The guard disguised in a tuxedo and masquerade mask came up and claimed his prize.

"Let's go back to the lounge," he said. He held her hand up to do a little twirl. And as she spun, he smacked her ass with his paddle.

Nice extra touch there.

"Now we're getting some mentions," said the director into my ear.

"What are people saying?" I replied.

"Let's see:

"Is this a #Odegaard fashion show or an auction? I'm confused.

"Is anyone watching this #Odegaard fashion show? Are they auctioning the clothes or the girls?

"Is that the same mask that they use in those banana party pornos? #Odegaard

"Why do these #Odegaard models all have bags on their heads???

"Did that #Odegaard bikini just sell for 300 grand?

"OMG that guy just smacked that #Odegaard model's ass with his paddle. What is happening?"

Perfect. "Have our graphics guys turn that ass smack into a gif. I want that shit trending before the next model sells."

"Already on it."

Model #3 sold to another one of my guards for 250K. And then Model #4 sold for 175K. They also took their models through the double doors at the back of the auditorium and into the lounge.

As the door swung shut, I definitely caught a glimpse of model #2 bent over a couch. I couldn't see what was happening behind her, but based on the way her tits were bouncing everywhere, I had a feeling she was getting fucked.

"Did you just broadcast that?" I asked into my earpiece.

"What?"

"The view of the lounge when the door opened."

"I think so. Why? Oh shit. Never mind. Someone just posted a gif of it."

Yes!

"Mentions are skyrocketing. But no spike on the website yet."

"Damn it. What are people saying?" I asked.

"Holy shit! One of the models at the #Odegaard show is definitely getting fucked backstage.

"Yup. Definitely a #Odegaard sex auction.

"lol @ the #Odegaard model getting fucked with the bag still on her head. This shit is wild."

"Any more mentions of my mask?" I asked.

"A few more people have mentioned it. But it's not the headline."

Shit. "Have one of our squads put on some monkey masks and take over cabana #1. And give all the guards in the lounge monkey masks too. We probably have less than

60 seconds until the producers at *Entertainment Miami* realize that they just aired footage of a girl getting railed."

If we couldn't get people going to the banana party website before *Entertainment Miami* pulled the plug, this plan would be dead in the water. And then I'd be literally dead in the water, courtesy of Mr. Locatelli's favorite hitman.

Model #5 strutted out onto stage. Chastity's tan friend with the great ass. And her ass looked even better than before now that she was all dressed up in her bikini. Justin must have used some sort of fancy glitter lotion, because her ass was literally sparkling.

The first four girls had done a decent job. But this girl walked like a professional supermodel. She attacked every step, timing it just right to make all her fun bits jiggle.

Was she a famous model? It wouldn't have surprised me if she was. Chastity probably had lots of model friends back in NYC. I stared at her ass, mentally comparing it to all the asses in this year's *Sports Illustrated* Swimsuit Issue.

Nope... Definitely not a real model. Because she forgot to stop at the end of the runway.

She just stepped right off the glass and into the sand. And then she marched right up to cabana #1, dropped to her knees, unbuttoned the bottom half of her veil, and started sucking one of the guard's cocks.

Holy shit! "Put up the error screen," I said. We'd prepared an error screen with a picture of a construction worker in a monkey mask, a little blurb about technical difficulties, and the URL for the banana party website.

"Roger that," said the director. "Shit. They pulled the feed."

"Did the error screen get up in time?"

"Umm... I'm not sure. It was definitely close. Nope...never mind."

"They didn't show it?"

"Oh no. They showed it. Just for a second. And it's blowing up on twitter. #OdegaardBananaParty is trending."

Fuck yes. "Go live on the website."

"Going live in three, two, one. And we're live. Ten thousand viewers and counting."

Beautiful.

"Ladies and gentleman of the internet," I said into the nearest camera. "Welcome to the world's first live sex auction."

Chapter 23

SELLING THE VIRGIN

The events of Sunday, Sept 22, 2013, as told by the

banana king

"The entire show will be completely free to view," I said. "But if you'd like to help choose the fate of our beautiful models, I invite you to bid on the options on the right side of your screen." Now I just had to figure out what to have them bid on…

Cheers erupted from the buyers as the guard at cabana #1 blasted Chastity's friend with a thick load of cum. His white cum really stood out on the black fabric. And it looked even better dripping down onto her tan tits.

Lucky bastard.

Although he wasn't that lucky. Because he wasn't going to get to fuck Ash tonight. And I was.

When the guard was finished cumming on her, the model stood up, spun around, and walked straight back down the runway with the same ferocity as before. As if she hadn't just given some random dude a blowjob.

I tried to grab her leash as she walked by me, but she tugged it away from me and whipped my hand with it. And then she walked off stage.

What the hell?

"Did you tell her to do that?" I asked into my earpiece.

"No, sir. We just told her to go walk the runway and then go back to you to get auctioned."

So she wanted to blow some random guard? But she didn't want to get auctioned? I was so confused. And kind of intrigued. But for now…the show had to go on.

"Okay," I said. "I hope you all enjoyed that little teaser. Now it's your turn to be in control." I looked over at Chastity on the side of the stage. She had one hand on her hip while she twirled her leash with her other, seemingly not giving a single fuck that she was about to get auctioned. It was the hottest I'd ever seen her look. Probably because there was a bag covering her face. Don't get me wrong – she was beautiful. But when I couldn't see her face, it was easy to just focus on her tits and forget that she was my mortal enemy.

"Our next model is recently engaged. So my first question to you, good people of the internet, is… Should we let her fiancé know that his girl is about to get auctioned?"

The options *yes* and *no* appeared on the three-story-tall screen behind me. A timer next to the options started counting down from thirty seconds.

"This is a tough choice," I said to the live audience. "Part of me thinks *no* is the better option. I mean…it seems rude to make the poor guy watch his fiancée get auctioned to the highest bidder. But in defense of choosing *yes*, it does seem a bit unsporting to auction a man's fiancée without giving him a chance to buy her. This could actually be a beautiful moment in their relationship if he outbids the entire internet to keep her pussy all to himself."

I looked back at the screen. Ten seconds left.

"Either way, it's not up to me. Just a few more seconds to get your final votes in. And…time's up! Let's see what you've chosen."

Two bars appeared on the screen next to *yes* and *no*. Each bar had $0 written next to it. And then we began revealing the bids. Both bars grew together at first as the numbers ticked up into the thousands. Then *no* got out to a bit of a lead. But eventually *yes* took the victory, $15,023 to about $8,000.

Excellent choice. I couldn't wait to fuck with her fiancé, Chad Chadwick. And if things went well, maybe this would break them up. Having a marriage alliance between the Morgans and Chadwicks would be quite bad for business.

But none of that would matter if I couldn't get people to bid more. Only $15K for the winning vote wasn't going to cut it. Not even close. I needed to pivot…

"The yeses have it!" I announced. "Let's see if we can get in touch with him. But before we do, there are a few things I'd like to mention. First, our model can't hear anything that's being said. She only hears what the producer says into her ear. So she has no idea this is being broadcast to the world. And she definitely doesn't know that her fiancé will be watching. Should we keep it that way? Or should we tell her? And I'm not sure I mentioned this before, but you'll only be charged for your bid if you're part of the winning vote."

That was my pivot. It was a big risk. But I had a feeling that the prospect of not having to pay unless you were on the winning side would make people much more likely to vote.

The voting ended in a landslide for *no – don't tell her*. And the best part was that it had just earned me over $100,000. The pivot had worked!

"Alright…let's get her fiancé on the line." I pulled Chastity's phone out of my jacket pocket. It had been tough to find in the bachelorette suite. But eventually we'd found the phone that unlocked with her fingerprint. I opened her messages and scrolled down to her conversation with "Babe".

"Is the phone showing up for you?" I asked into my earpiece.

"Yup," confirmed the director. "I've added it to the live feed. Everyone can see your conversation."

Perfect.

"Hey babe," I texted. "Have you seen what's happening on bananaparty.com right now?"

His reply came almost immediately. "No…"

"OMG you have to check it out."

"K one sec." There was a pause. And then he texted again. "What the hell? Why is this conversation being broadcast?"

I waved to the camera. "Can you hear me?" I asked out loud rather than via text. "Text back if you can hear me."

"I can hear you, asshole. Where's my girl?"

"Just backstage. Want me to get her?"

"Yes."

"You got it. Send out the next model!"

Music started playing and Chastity strutted out on stage, just as professionally as her friend. If anything, Chastity was even more confident.

"We'll let you start the bidding, *babe*," I said as Chastity splashed down the runway.

"$100," was all he texted.

"A hundred dollars?" I asked. "That's all?"

"$200?" he responded. "That seems like a lot for a bikini."

I laughed. "Oh wow. You're not bidding on the bikini, dude. You're bidding on *her*."

"Are you serious?"

"Let me show you how serious I am."

Chastity had just finished her walk and was now standing next to me. So I reached behind her and unhooked her bikini top. She didn't even flinch as the fabric fell away from her tits.

"Whoa! What the fuck, man!" he texted. "Put those away."

"Sure thing. But first you need to outbid the entire internet."

"I'll give you $1,000 to stop this shit."

"Hmmm... Something tells me that won't be *quite* enough. But you're welcome to bid when the voting starts. Let's take a look at the other options."

"Showing all the bidders now," said the director in my ear as the wall-mounted cameras panned around the room from cabana to cabana.

"You have one minute to decide our lovely model's fate," I said to our audience. "The bidding starts...now!" I gave people a second to start bidding, and then I kept talking. "So what are we thinking? Should we take pity on her fiancé? Or should we all enjoy watching her tits bounce while she gets railed by a complete stranger?" I reached over and gave her tits a jiggle. "Wow. Look at these puppies. It's a rare thing to find such big, perky natural tits. And this ass..." I held her hand and spun her.

Chastity's phone buzzed.

"Get your hands off her," texted Chad. "I'm calling the police."

"Go right ahead," I said. "We have signed release forms on file from all of our models this evening. Annnnd...time's up! Let's see if her fiancé loves her enough to outbid the entire internet."

The options popped up on the screen behind me. The bar next to *Babe* started filling up first. But it only got to $1001 before it stopped.

"Wow," I said. "It's your lucky day, *babe*. It appears one other person was willing to donate a single dollar to keep your girl safe. But will that be enough?" I shook my head and laughed. "Definitely not."

The other bars started filling up. Everyone in the cabanas were listed as possibilities to fuck Chastity. But *Wolf Mask in Cabana #13* quickly rose to the top, easily surpassing the $1001 that *Babe* had received.

"Wow," I said as it ticked over $1,000,000.

The guy in the wolf mask from cabana #13 got up and started to walk towards stage, a camera man following him every step of the way. But then the bar next to *Woman in the Cat Mask in Cabana #3* started growing. And growing. And growing.

Interesting twist.

It finally stopped at over 1.1 million.

"It looks like we have a winner," I said. "*Babe*, how do you feel about that?"

"I don't love it," texted Chad. "But at least she's not gonna get fucked by a dick."

But then the chart started shifting again. Suddenly *Guard #2* shot to the very top with over 1.5 million.

Hell yes!

If the rest of this went according to plan, I could actually get the eight million that we needed.

"Oooh," I said. "Looks like I'd declared a winner a bit prematurely. Sorry about that, babe. Guard #2, come on up."

A guard in a monkey mask emerged from the corner and stepped onto stage. And I immediately knew why the internet had chosen him. His tuxedo pants were *very* clingy, making it quite obvious that he had a huge dick.

He gave both of Chastity's tits a nice squeeze.

"Hey," I said. "Hands off. The internet still has to choose what you get to do to her. Shall we see your options?"

The guard nodded and four options appeared on the screen.

"We've got tittyfuck her until he cums, bend her over on the runway, fuck her in the ass, and share her with the other guards. Which one are you hoping for?"

He stared at her tits. And then looked back at her ass. "Is there an option for all of the above?" he asked.

"Nope."

"Hmm…then I guess my choice would have to be to fuck her in the ass."

"Solid choice. What about you, *babe*. What are you hoping he does to her?"

"None of the above," texted Chad. "And it shouldn't be up for a vote, you sick fuck. It should be her choice."

"Fair enough. We can add those options."

Girl's choice and *None of the above* appeared on the screen.

"Let the voting begin!"

The music started again and Chastity walked to the end of the runway. I forgot to keep talking about the different options. I was too captivated by her jiggling tits.

"Time's up!" I called. "Let's see what you've chosen."

None of the above went up first, but it stopped at $1000 on the dot. Apparently Chad had lost the support of the one other person who didn't want her to get fucked. Then all the other options quickly overtook it.

Share her with the other guards went up next. All the way to 1.9 million. *Tittyfuck her until he cums* came on strong, but petered out at 434K. *Bend her over on the runway* and *Girl's choice* did slightly better, but still came nowhere near the gangbang. And then *Fuck her in the ass* came out of nowhere, rocketing all the way up to 2.3 million.

I was about to call it. But then *Girl's choice* made a late surge. One million. One point five. Two…

"Wow," I said. "It might be your lucky day, *babe*." And it was. Because even though it started to lose steam, *Girl's choice* had just enough votes to tick past the ass fucking. "Girl's choice it is! Guard #2, go ahead and walk the runway and we'll see what she chooses."

Chastity turned around to watch him walk towards her. He tore his shirt off halfway down the runway, exposing his chiseled eight pack. I'd seen those abs just a few hours ago. They belonged to Kendrick Jones, aka Birthmark.

Shit. I hope he can get hard again.

All my worries dissipated when he got to Chastity and ripped his pants off. His massive eleven-inch cock swung towards her, birthmark and all.

He took a step towards her.

This was the moment of truth. What would she choose to do with him?

Unfortunately for Chad, I had a feeling she was gonna choose to bend over for him. Or at least get titty fucked. There was no way Chastity would pass up such a big cock.

But as he stepped towards her, she put her hand on his chest and pushed him back. She shook her head no and gave him a sassy little finger waggle.

"Yeah!" texted Chad. "I knew she'd be loyal!"

His victory was short lived, though. Because Chastity looked to either side and motioned for the other guards to come join her. Their cocks were out by the time they reached the stage. And she was eager to bend over and grab them.

"So much for her being loyal," I said as Birthmark grabbed her thong and tore it off. And then he was inside of her. She arched her back and pressed against him, slowly taking all eleven inches. "Looks like she went for the sharing option."

Chad didn't send any more texts. He'd probably thrown his phone across the room. Or maybe he was enjoying the show.

And what a show it was. Birthmark had gotten some nice practice with Maeve, so he knew just how to use her leash to get maximum thrust power. And Chastity's gloves were already starting to rip from jerking off the other four guards.

Originally I'd thought it was bad when Maeve's gloves had ripped so easily. But now I'd decided that was more of a feature than a flaw. It was fucking hot when a girl was so horny that she didn't even care when her diamond-studded gloves started to rip.

Eventually one of the guys picked her up over his shoulder and carried her into the lounge. All the other guards and a few camera men followed.

"We'll check back in on them soon," I said as the doors swung shut. "But first…it's time for the main event. Ladies and gentlemen of the internet, I present to you…our virgin!"

My dick stiffened in its sleeve as Ash walked out onto stage in her little white bikini. The diamonds on the gloves and the garter and her shoes sparkled under the bright lights. But I was focused solely on her virgin pussy. I wanted to tear her thong off and take her right then and there. And then, just as I claimed her, I'd tear the bag off her head so I could see the look on her face.

Unfortunately, we'd only earned a little over four million dollars so far. And we needed double that.

"Unlike our previous model's fiancé, our virgin's father is a very rich man. And he's willing to pay five million dollars to keep her virginity intact," I lied. I had no idea who

Ash's parents were, but I was pretty sure they didn't have that kind of money. "If you can bid more than that by the time she gets back to the stage, then her virginity is ours."

The screen turned into an empty bar, slowly filling towards the five-million-dollar mark.

And by slowly…I mean pretty damned quickly.

Ash had just struck a pose at the end of the runway, and we were already at 2 million.

Up and up it went. But she was almost back to the stage and we were still only at 3.5 million.

"Getting close," I said. "I should probably show you what she'll be losing her virginity to." I motioned a camera man over. And with the camera pointed right at my junk, I tore off my tuxedo pants, revealing my massive cock to everyone.

Including Ash…who got so distracted by it that she tripped and fell. The sharks circled below, and I couldn't blame them. Her tits had popped out when she fell, and they were magnificent.

She slowly got back to her feet and finished walking to the stage with her hands covering her perfect tits. Just as she stepped off the glass, the bar filled up to five million dollars.

YES!!!

All the high-rollers in the cabanas cheered.

"Why is everyone cheering?" she asked through the bag on her head.

"Because your virginity is mine."

The skin on her chest flushed. And I was sure her face was bright red too.

I probably should have let the internet vote on what position I took her in. But I'd already gotten enough money, so the choice was all mine.

I grabbed her leash and led her back to the lounge.

Wow. I'd forgotten that all the other models were back here getting fucked.

Two of them were bent over a leather couch getting fucked from behind while a camera man captured the whole thing. Another had taken the bag off her head and was getting spit roasted by a guard and a cameraman. She stared directly into the camera as she greedily took his entire cock down her throat. And Chastity was riding Birthmark's cock in the middle of the room while she stroked two other cocks. She'd unbuttoned the bottom half of the bag on her head so she could suck another.

I led Ash over to a round loveseat and pushed her onto her back. She propped herself up on her elbows and spread her legs. Two camera men rushed over, eager to capture the grand finale for our audience.

"Good girl," I muttered as I tore Ash's thong off.

She let out a little yelp.

God, her virgin pussy was beautiful. I wanted nothing more than to claim it, but I had to take my time so I didn't kill the poor girl with my huge cock.

I knelt down and pushed my monkey mask up a bit so that I could slowly kiss up her legs, starting with her ankle.

Her skin was so soft beneath my lips. And it got softer the closer I got to her eager pussy.

She was so wet that she was dripping. I ran my tongue the rest of the way up her inner thigh, tasting her for the first time. I nearly came when my tongue lapped up her juices. *Nearly*. I thrust my tongue into her wetness to get more.

She tasted like sweet honey. And I couldn't get enough. I thrust my tongue deeper, burying my face against her pussy.

She grabbed the back of my head.

I knew she was a greedy girl.

I moved my mouth to her clit and slid a finger inside of her. And then another. And then another. If she couldn't handle three fingers, there was no way she'd be able to handle my cock. She kept thrusting her hips towards my face, her panting growing louder. But I wasn't going to let her come just yet. I wanted her first orgasm to be around my thick cock.

I couldn't wait any longer. I swirled my tongue around her clit one more time and jammed a fourth finger inside of her tight pussy. She could *just* take it.

"Ready for this?" I asked as I rubbed her juices onto my cock.

She nodded.

Fucking finally!

I'd been waiting for this moment all day. I glanced at one of the cameras mounted in the corner of the room. The internet was going to love this. I turned back to Ash.

I pushed the tip of my cock against her soft pussy.

Should I pull the bag off her head now? No. Not yet. I wanted to wait until just the right moment…

Ash moaned as the tip of my cock disappeared inside of her. And then, inch by inch, I claimed her virgin pussy.

Almost there…

"Oh fuck," she moaned. "I don't know how much more I can take."

Three more inches to go.

And I knew she could take it all. She'd practically been begging me to fill her ever since I'd kidnapped her.

I grabbed her hips with one hand and grabbed the bag on her head with my other hand.

And then, in one swift motion, I slammed into her and pulled the bag off her head.

"Fuuuuuuck!" she screamed. Her face was pure ecstasy as her entire body shook.

"What the fuck?" I asked. "Who are you?" Because the girl I was staring down at was an extremely hot redhead. But she wasn't Ash.

WHAT REALLY HAPPENED
Saturday - Oct 10, 2026

Ash stared in disbelief at the recording. "Wait… So the banana king *didn't* take my virginity?"

"Nope! He fucked Autumn instead. Sexy twin gambit for the win!"

"But how? We got caught by those guards…"

I shook my head. "I never said that."

"Yes you did! I totally blew our cover after dick, dick, dick, right?

"Yeah. Poker tried to grab you, but you were covered in so much cum that he just slipped right off. Slavanka round-house-kicked Rookie while Sloane took down Bandit. The other guards that you and Autumn had sucked off were still handcuffed so they were pretty useless."

"But I saw the security footage of us being marched into the lobby by the guards."

"Correction: You saw the security footage of *us* dressed as guards marching our doppelgängers into the lobby. Thank God that short king finally arrived or we never would have been able to find a guard outfit for your tiny little body. And I still can't get over the fact that the banana king command-ed us to walk right out the front door of his resort. Just like I'd promised him he would."

"Holy shit, Chastity. You're a freaking genius!"

"Are you just realizing this now?"

"No. I've known that. But this rescue plan was next level. Well played." Ash reached out and honked my boobs *three* times. "I know you're allowed a max of two boob squeezes to compliment a good outfit, but I think you should be allowed a third to thank your bestie for coming up with an epic plan to save you from a dirty kidnapper."

"That seems fair."

"Wait!" She suddenly looked horrified. "Our poor doppelgängers got auctioned off. And the whole thing got broadcast all over the world."

"Yeah it did!"

"Those poor girls. I can't believe we kidnapped them to save ourselves. I take back those three boob grabs. You're a monster."

I laughed. "We didn't kidnap anyone. They were excited to do it."

"There's no way Autumn would have been okay getting fucked on camera in front of the entire world."

"Uhhh… Are you sure about that? Because that girl *loves* dick. As soon as I told her I could get her fucked by a foot-long cock she was totally down to get auctioned. She was actually the most agreeable of the three. Granted…none of them realized it was going to be broadcast to the whole world. But it worked out great in the end. They're all living their best lives now."

Ash looked so excited. "Autumn was able to leverage her 15 minutes of whore-fame into getting invited to the pro circuit of Trivial Pursuit?! I had a feeling she had it in her…"

"What? No. She divorced her cheating husband. And while she was thrilled to finally get that foot-long dick that she'd always dreamed of, she ultimately decided that it was too big for daily use. The next weekend she invited Poker to a game night, and the rest is history. Now they're happily married."

"No way."

"Yes way. We'll actually see them at the wedding in a few minutes when we land."

"For real?" She looked so excited.

"Yup. I can't believe you didn't keep in touch with your doppelgänger. I talk to mine at least once a week."

"How could I have kept in touch with her? I didn't even remember she existed until like ten minutes ago!"

"Fair point."

"So what happened to Chloe and Sloane?" Ash's mouth dropped open. "Oh my God! It just hit me that the banana king had been talking to Chloe's fiancé rather than Chad during the auction. And it seemed totally in character for Slavanka to randomly blow that guard at the end of the runway. But Sloane was a fancy princess, right? Her parents must have disowned her so hard after that."

"They did. But she got super famous in the fashion world for that runway blowjob that she gave. She was invited to walk for some of the biggest names in fashion, and now she has her own super successful label. Maybe after I get back from my honeymoon we can go to one of her shows. It's always exciting to see which one of her models will give an audience member a blowjob."

Ash laughed. "And Chloe?"

"Happily married."

"To…who?"

"Harrison. Who else?"

"The same Harrison she was engaged to that weekend? The fiancé who watched her get gangbanged at that auction?"

"Yup!"

"I don't believe you."

"I'll prove it." I grabbed my phone off the table and videochatted Chloe.

Harrison answered. He was looking quite handsome in his tuxedo.

"Hey, Harrison," I said.

"Ah! Chastity! I'm so excited for your wedding!"

"Me too!" I squealed. "Is Chloe there?"

"She should be down any minute." He checked his watch. "I don't know what's taking her so long. She's been getting ready forever. Let's go check on her…" He switched the camera so that it was pointed out ahead of him as he walked to the bathroom of their hotel suite.

He gave a light knock on the door and Chloe called, "Come in!"

Harrison opened the door and…

Chloe looked about…half ready. She had her hair all curled. And her jewelry was on. But she was full nude. And crouching in the middle of the bathroom sucking a huge cock.

"Oh my God," gasped Ash.

"Hey babe," said Chloe. "I'll be down in… Are you filming this? You naughty boy."

"It's Chastity," said Harrison.

"Oh! Hi, Chastity! I promise I'm not gonna be late to your wedding. My face was just looking a little dry so I asked Bandit if he could give me a quick facial."

"Good call," I said. "I won't keep you. See you soon!" I blew her a kiss and ended the call. I turned to Ash. "See? Happily married."

Ash looked so surprised. "Does she follow the…" She clasped her hand over her mouth. "I mean…what was going on there?!" she said, sounding EXTREMELY shocked. Like…too shocked. Almost like she wasn't shocked at all.

I'd dig into that more later. "Watching the auction made Harrison realize that he really liked watching Chloe with other men. Which worked out great, because Chloe needed more excitement in the bedroom. He surprised her on their honeymoon by asking their well-endowed butler to fuck her, and ever since then Chloe and Harrison have been one of the happiest couples I've ever known."

"Weird," said Ash, but it didn't seem like she actually thought it was that weird.

I stared at her. What had she been about to ask before she clasped her hand over her mouth?

Ash cleared her throat. "Wait. You were fighting with Ghostie. What happened with that?"

I laughed. "You know what happened with that."

"No I don't. And he was really mad at you. He wanted you all to himself and you kept sharing your cooch with everyone." She gestured toward my lap. She was clearly trying to change the subject because she knew I was suspicious of her. And she was starting to sweat profusely. Girl definitely had a secret she was keeping from me.

I just stared at her. "He clearly forgave me."

"I don't think so."

I laughed. "He obviously did."

"Mhm." Her voice squeaked awkwardly as sweat dripped from her brow.

Okay, enough. I wanted to know what she'd been about to say earlier. Besides, if I didn't intervene she was going to turn into a puddle. And there was only one way to get the truth out of her…

I walked over to the minibar, but there was no banana juice.

Damn it!

I slammed the door shut. I was going to have to talk to shmoopie poo about his liquor selection on his private jet. This was unacceptable.

Luckily, though, I always followed the updated version of Single Girl Rule #5: Have banana juice in your purse at all times.

I pulled my flask out of my purse and handed it to Ash.

"No way," said Ash, shaking her head. "I obviously can't be trusted when I've had banana juice."

"But…it's my wedding day. So you have to!"

"That's not one of the single girl rules. And anyway. I'm a married girl now. So I have…not to follow those crazy rules anymore."

That was a weird way to phrase that.

"Please?" I asked.

"No."

"Then I guess you'll never know who took your virginity." I sighed. "Which is a real shame. You would freak the fuck out if you knew who took it."

"I'm not falling for this again. You're just going to tell me some long ass story about me drinking banana juice and blowing a bunch of dudes. And then I'm not gonna lose my V-card. I'm pretty sure you're just fucking with me and I never actually had sex with anyone before I got married."

I stared at her. "Girl…"

"Girl," she replied.

"You were definitely not a virgin when you got married."

"Then tell me the real story!"

I pushed the flask of banana juice across the table.

"Gah, fine. But this better be good!" She grabbed the flask and took a big swig.

By the time I finished this story, she'd be drunk enough to tell me whatever weird secret she was keeping. "Okay, so…three months later…"

"Three months? What happened during the rest of our first semester of college?"

"Very little, really. You hardly left our dorm all semester. You had this very odd paranoia about being kidnapped. Which is strange to me now since you clearly didn't remember it happening."

"Damn it, Chastity! Why didn't you just start three months into the story if that's when I lost my virginity?"

"Because backstory is important. I had to show your character development."

"What character development?!" asked Ash. "My entire character in this story is that I love sucking dick."

"Exactly. And you didn't know it before. You just assumed it was a new development once you met your husband. But you've always loved that D." I went to give her a high five.

And since she'd had a sip of banana-juice…she happily high fived me back.

"Now tell me the story," she said. "And make sure you cut to the good part, because I'm not getting off this plane until I know who took my V-card. I don't care if it makes me late to your wedding." She shifted uncomfortably.

"I don't believe that for one second," I said. "I can see you already sweating again at the thought of being late. But I promise this'll be quick. It all started a couple days before Christmas when I invited you to a ski resort for the annual meeting of the families…"

What's Next?

This is it. Ash is losing her virginity for Christmas. I promise it's happening this time!

Read Single Girl Rules #HoHoHo to see who takes it.

Get your copy today!

The Society

#STALKERPROBLEMS

You know that Chastity is going to get her man (or men…), but what about poor, sweet Ash?

Well I have some good news… Ash has an entire series all about her wild journey to find love! And you better believe Chastity is gonna be there every step of the way to help her.

And yes, Ash is definitely going to still be abiding by the Single Girl Rules. In fact, in the Society, you'll learn about at least 10 more of the rules.

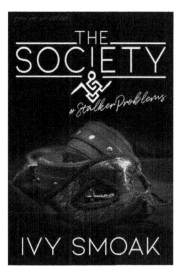

I got an invitation to an illicit club.

They say they'll grant me three wishes.

They say they'll make all my wildest dreams come true.

All I have to do is sign the contract.

Is it too good to be true? I'm about to find out.

Get your copy today!

A Note From Ivy

Gah! Who the heck does Ash lose her virginity to?!

Well, I have good news. I'm finally answering that question in the next installment - Single Girl Rules #HoHoHo! And yes, it's a Christmas story! And yes, it's much more naughty than nice. Actually it's only naughty. You'll probably end up on the naughty list just reading it ;)

And I have to agree with Chastity here. You gotta show all the steamy details along the way. And there aren't many things steamier than the Locatelli's finest guards. After all, the banana king only hires men with 8 abs and 8 inches at his resorts. Who else would want to be part of that sex auction? Unless a small-dicked oligarch bids on you of course. #BooTinyPenises. You know you'd go for at least a million though ;)

Also, is anyone else obsessed with learning more about the Single Boy Rules and the banana king? There is definitely more of him coming. Wait! Does that mean *HE* is the one that finally takes Ash's virginity in the next book? Hmm… If so, I hope she doesn't tear in two.

And who else thought they got some hints about who Chastity marries from the scenes in the private jet?

Ivy Smoak

Ivy Smoak
Wilmington, DE
www.ivysmoak.com

About the Author

Ivy Smoak is the Wall Street Journal, USA Today, and Amazon #1 bestselling author of *The Hunted Series*. Her books have sold over 4 million copies worldwide.

When she's not writing, you can find Ivy binge watching too many TV shows, taking long walks, playing outside, and generally refusing to act like an adult. She lives with her husband in Delaware.

TikTok: @IvySmoak
Facebook: IvySmoakAuthor
Instagram: @IvySmoakAuthor
Goodreads: IvySmoak

Printed in Great Britain
by Amazon